A FLYTE OF PAPER DARTS

A FLYTE OF PAPER DARTS

John Millican

Book Guild Publishing

Sussex, England

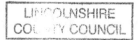
First published in Great Britain in 2005 by
The Book Guild Ltd
25 High Street
Lewes, East Sussex
BN7 2LU

Typesetting in Baskerville by
SetSystems Ltd, Saffron Walden, Essex

Printed in Great Britain by
CPI Bath

A catalogue record for this book is
available from the British Library

ISBN 1 85776 965 1

To Rae

Contents

'Digressions, incontestably, are the sunshine;
they are the life, the soul of reading.'

Laurence Sterne, *Tristram Shandy*

Part 1

How the Hunt Started

The murder of Roger Boyle will not greatly concern us. He would probably have been murdered anyway, if not in Loocestershire then somewhere else. He was that sort of man. It was not murder that engaged the devious mind of Potter and challenged Grue's inexorable will. It was what followed when Constable Tidd crossed a bridge on Ethelralda's Eve.

Some say that Ethelralda was that bad-tempered Druid of whom Giraldus Cambrensis relates that he sat upon a heap of cold wet stones prophesying in a sniffiness of Welsh dire things to any who would listen or to the great sea itself. Others hold that he was an Irish saint who discovered America in a coracle and thereafter retired to merited martyrdom in Loocestershire – Loo, as it then was called. (In the country of the Basques they tell the same story of St Pée.) Whatever the truth of the matter, it is a curious fact that Loocestershire folks fear to pass water on Ethelralda's Eve.

Hence the unease of Constable Tidd where, cold in the moonlight, the bridge humps across the canal. Three times an owl shrieked, bird of doom. *Tap-tap, tap-tap*, a stick upon the road. *Tap-tap*. Tidd's knees were knocking. He shone his torch.

It was but shepherd Grinder. About his waist hung rabbits, around his neck coiled wires.

1

'You be a honest man, Mr Grinder,' the constable quavered. 'Will ye go wi' me on the business o' the King?'

' 'Tis a Queen now, Mr Tidd.'

'More reason that her peace be kept. See yonder.' Tidd pointed to where a dark shape crouched amongst the soughing trees. 'Regular he comes. And waits.'

'Think you it be robbers, Mr Tidd? Or be it Russian spies?'

'Who can tell, Mr Grinder, and I fear to cross the water on this night.'

'I will go with you, Mr Tidd. No Primitive Methodist shall lack the help of Joel Grinder in time of need. But where be Constable Herring?'

'Be in haystack down the road wi' Dilsie Creepin' Mouse.'

'Arrr!' Grinder gargled noises of Old England then boldly they crossed the bridge. From the dark shape in the lane sounds scraped and noises shuffled. 'Shine your light, Mr Tidd,' advised the shepherd.

The beam shone on a Ford car, such as was favoured by district nurses. The seats in front were empty but on the back of one there was a foot. It twitched.

'Shine that light inside, Mr Tidd,' urged the shepherd. 'Let's see what the rogues are at!'

The beam probed over two figures which were disentangling in the back. The foot in front became a leg. Two legs. All that belonged to a whole body. The door swung open and the body reversed out with angry noises.

With that sweeping motion across the chest by which is known the authority of a policeman Tidd brought out notebook and laborious pencil stub. 'Kindly show your licence, sir,' he requested.

Coarse words answered this polite request, one particularly inappropriate.

2

'Watch your language, sir,' remonstrated Tidd. 'Hereabout we're chapel folk and there is a lady present.'

'Three times,' roared the angry figure. 'Three times you've asked me for my improper licence here, improper you!'

'Licentious!' breathed the shepherd, leaning closer to observe the wriggles of the female figure in the back. The lady shrieked at the intrusive whiskered face.

Unseen, two dark figures hurried over the bridge. They had sacks upon their shoulders.

'Bound to happen sometime, sir. Law of averages.'

'My house is not an average house!'

The Chief Constable's house had been burgled and all his silver stolen. It was the first burglary the county had seen in years. A retired military man, he had, between a bristle of moustache and a prominence of teeth, that stiff upper lip which foreigners attribute to the English national constipation. He normally greeted all and each with undifferentiating particularity: 'Good morning chew' – a tight emission which might have been to recommend some breakfast cereal. But that morning it was a declaration of savage intent. It spurted at the constable, spattered the sergeant and covered Grue with contumely.

'A whole week gone and you've got nowhere!'

'Yes sir, no sir.'

'Some of that silver's been in my family for generations!'

'Yes sir, no sir, three bags full.' Grue studied tea-leaves in an empty cup.

'And this, what's this?' The Chief Constable slammed down a letter on Grue's desk. It bore the heading of the town's university with the typed sub-heading 'Department of Manuscripts'.

Dear Sir,

When asked for my driving licence for the third time in as many weeks and in the same place, I swore at two policemen. Will you kindly convey my apologies to these officers. The incidents took place in Smeeton Lane. Doubtless they were only doing their duty.

Yours faithfully,

Amadeus Potter

'Just another complaint, sir.'

'Complaint? The fellow's apologising.'

'Nobody sends us apologies.'

The Chief Constable picked the letter up. 'Seems a decent enough letter to me. What's it all about?'

Grue consulted records. 'Ah yes, the gold.'

'Gold? What gold? It's silver we're concerned about.'

'Quite so, sir; but this has nothing to do with the burglary of your house. We had a circular about stolen gold.'

'Nothing about gold in Potter's letter.'

'No sir. Mr Potter wouldn't know about that.'

'Then what the devil has it to do with Potter's apology?'

'The constables had been told to keep their eyes open when they were in Westerby, watch for strangers, anything suspicious. That's where the gold thief used to live. They saw a car parked without lights in the lane and went to investigate. What they found was Potter in the back with a girl.'

'But three times the letter says. Three times, Grue!'

'Yes sir, Mr Potter does seem to be a man of regular habits. I'll have a word with our zealous constables. I shouldn't think you need to concern yourself further in the matter.'

'I shall though, I'll write to Potter. It is public-spirited of him to apologise. Respect for authority should be encouraged – far too little of it these days. Burglaries and these hippy fellows all over the place. Fellow even shouted at the Hunt last week. Know what he said?'

'Can't imagine, sir.'

'"Get your damn dogs off the road!"' The Chief Constable waved his swizzle-stick, as he did when particularly agitated. '"Get your damn dogs off the road!" Stuck his head out of the car window and shouted at us! He'd had to pull in to the verge to let us pass, but chaps gave him a wave with their whips and some of the ladies nodded. Shouted at us. Sort of fellow who might have burgled my house. Shouldn't be surprised if it was him. One of these district-nurse Fords. You keep your eye open for a hippy in a district-nurse Ford.'

'Right sir. District-nurse Ford.'

'And I'll write to this Potter.'

'Should settle the matter, sir.'

It would have, but for Roger Boyle. It was a few days later when Grue telephoned the Chief Constable with the startling news.

'Ah, good morning t'you, Inspector. You've found my silver?'

'No sir, we have a murder on our hands.'

'Good heavens!'

'You remember, sir, that letter you received from Mr Potter.'

'Indeed I do, a very decent letter. And now you tell me that the poor fellow's been murdered?'

'No, not him. But it was in his house that the murder was committed.'

'What does he know about it? Did he do it?'

'He didn't do it but he knows more than he is letting on. The murdered man was called Boyle. Seems to have been living abroad, and was staying in the Salvation Army hostel here.'

'Was he a musician? Trombone, that sort of thing?'

'No musical instrument in his luggage, nothing of interest except his passport. He had broken into the house and was probably killed by some confederate. The crime was discovered by our constables when they saw the broken windows from the garden. It's the house where the gold thief lived, you see. Potter bought it.'

'Potter knew the gold thief then?'

'I don't believe he knew the gold thief but he did know Boyle. I have him in one of the cells, kept him overnight. I'll be questioning him again shortly.'

'This Boyle – could he be the one who stole my silver? Or Potter, could it have been Potter? Bear the possibility in mind, Grue. And keep me informed. Good morning t'you.' The Chief Constable waved his swizzle-stick in dismissal and went back to his interrupted breakfast and his reading of *Horse and Hound.*

On the night of the murder Potter had been at a party and it would have been about two o'clock in the morning when he got back to Westerby and drove cautiously down the street. There were two cars outside his house, which was a nuisance, and they had their lights on, which was careless, and the light was on in his house too. Careless, very careless. Carelessness costs lives.

And the key wouldn't turn in the lock, which was absurd. He might have forgotten to lock off the light but certainly he had switched on the key. Absurd.

And then the lock snicked by itself. The door opened. 'It wasn't locked,' said a large policeman. 'Come in.'

Bloody cheek! Potter stamped in. There were two more

of them. They had his teapot on the table, and cups and milk and sugar.

'You've been having a bloody tea-party in my house!' shouted Potter.

'We have been waiting for quite a time. Where have you been for the past few hours, Mr Potter?' The one who spoke was in plain clothes. 'I am Inspector Grue.'

'Been? Where have I been? Where I've every right to been – which is more than you can say. How did you get in here?'

'There are certain useful arts which the police have learned from the criminal classes, Mr Potter.' The Inspector nodded and one policeman went to stand with his back to the kitchen door. Another stood against the door to the street.

The third sat at the table with a notebook. The Inspector went to lean on the back of Potter's armchair. 'You have not answered my question. And here's another. Do you know this man?'

The one in the armchair was also in plain clothes. It was the impudent fellow who had spoken to him beside the canal, the same bovine stare.

'Boyle,' said Potter. 'His name is Boyle.'

'So you knew him. A friend, would you say?' The Inspector's eyes lifted to meet Potter's. 'Or an enemy perhaps?'

It was then that Potter saw the blood. 'What . . . what's wrong with him?'

'He's dead, Mr Potter. Now how do you explain that?'

'He can't be dead!'

The Inspector looked down dispassionately. 'It is the normal consequence of murder.'

'Murder? In my house?'

'So now tell me, Mr Potter, where have you been for the past few hours?'

Potter sank down on to a chair at the table. He was feeling sick. 'A party. I've been at a party.'

'And where was this party?'

Potter clasped the teapot with both hands. A friend. He muttered an address. The Inspector nodded to the uniforms and they went out into the street. Potter's eyes were everywhere except on that figure in the armchair.

'Don't try to escape,' the Inspector grunted. 'You won't get far.'

The kitchen door opened. The man who came in was wiping red-stained hands on Potter's kitchen towel. He tossed it back through the door behind him. 'This the tenant?'

'The owner.'

'Looks a bit queasy.'

'He's been at a party. Or so he says.'

The man who had joined them peered closely into Potter's face. 'I'd better wash my hands.' He went back into the kitchen. There was the sound of running water. Shortly he returned carrying a black bag. 'Good strawberries in the garden, Grue. You should try them.' He dropped his bag on the table, pushing teapot and cups aside. A bottle was unscrewed, pills fell on to the table. One rolled off. The bagman cursed and scrabbled and held it out to Potter. 'Swallow.'

The bag clicked shut as Potter swallowed. 'I'm off then, Grue. No more corpses tonight, mm?' He consulted a pocket watch. 'Or this morning, to be more precise.' The street door banged behind him.

A car started up and, as it drove off, another car screeched to a stop. The door banged open again. More men hurried in with cameras and other apparatus.

'Look around, Mr Potter,' said the Inspector. 'See if anything is missing. You'll only be in the way here. But don't try to run away.'

8

Potter had seen already that his papers and books were lying on the floor. In the kitchen there was broken glass, the window had been smashed. Upstairs he found clothes strewn about, and sheets and blankets. The mattress had been slashed, half the stuffing pulled out. Potter stumbled back downstairs and got outside before being sick.

The Inspector came and watched, his face a grey grimace in the light from the broken window, a tall man, gaunt. He grunted, went down the garden path and came back with a handful of strawberries.

By the time Potter had got his stomach under control the uniforms were back. The Inspector looked up from a sheet of paper. 'So you have an alibi. There are questions still to answer, though.' The Inspector glanced around. 'You can make a statement at the police station. You can hardly stay here anyway.'

The man in the armchair gawped at them from amongst puffs of powder and the flash of light bulbs, like someone waiting to be interviewed on television.

At the police station Potter answered questions. 'Sign,' said the Inspector when the typewriter had stopped chattering. Potter signed. 'Read it,' said the Inspector. Potter read it and signed again. All he wanted was to lie down and sleep.

After phoning the Chief Constable in the morning Grue called the duty constable. 'Potter awake?'

'Having breakfast now, sir.'

'Bring him when he's finished.'

Grue was reading from the record book when Potter was brought in, a dishevelled little man rubbing his back.

'You've had your breakfast, Mr Potter, so you needn't keep on being sore about our tea-party in your house.'

'That's not what I'm sore about.' Potter moved his torso around and flapped his arms. 'Bloody hell!'

9

Grue grunted. 'The government does not go out of its way to provide comforts for criminals. Or for the police. Sit down.'

Potter lowered himself carefully on to a bentwood chair. 'I've things to see to at the University.'

'You'll be taken there in a police car, but first we'll go over a few points.'

'Again?'

'Not about last night. About the night when you swore at two policemen. There's no connection with the murder – as far as I know – but from what you have told me I gather that the events of that night led you to buy your house. The police have been concerned with that house before – for reasons that I cannot tell you – and now again it comes to our attention. I have the record here.' Grue put his hand on a big black book. He opened it. His finger began to move across a page. 'Tell me all, well not all. We can omit ... hm ... and we can pass over ... hm ... Tell me what happened when you left Smeeton Lane.'

Potter had watched the moving finger uneasily. 'I wrote to apologise. I wrote to the Chief Constable. To apologise.'

Grue grimaced. 'Ah yes, your apology. But that was later. What happened that same night?'

'Nothing much. We went to the pub, the pub in Westerby. The girl ... she was upset so I took her to the pub. To have a drink.'

'Very natural. I suppose the young lady would be upset. A disagreeable experience. Your own experience is perhaps ... wider? But we needn't go into that. So you went to the pub and they told you about the house being for sale, and that is what I find surprising. They don't like strangers in the village. I wonder why they were so forthcoming on this occasion.'

'Well, they thought I had been helpful.'

'In what way, helpful?'

10

Potter stirred uncomfortably in his chair. 'There was a bit of a row, you see.'

'What sort of a row?'

'Do we have to go into all this?' Potter was looking at the big black book.

Grue closed it. 'Quite off the record, Mr Potter.'

'It was some hippies who caused it all . . .' Potter hesitated.

'Go on, Mr Potter. Caused what?'

'Well, there was a funny atmosphere when we went in. The locals were all bunched at the door and muttering together. Up at the far end there were three long-haired fellows in fancy gear, obviously not locals. They'd taken over the dartboard and they'd chalked their ban-the-bomb sign on the scoreboard and they were making a lot of noise. It's quite a quiet place usually, old-fashioned. Horse brasses, pewter pots, copper warming pans. Fox-hunting country about there.'

'Fox-hunter are you, Mr Potter?'

'Well no. But I like to see the Hunt go by. All right except for their yapping dogs and horrid little girls on ponies.'

'Dogs. The Chief Constable's after me about someone who swore at their dogs, fellow with a car just like yours.' Grue's hand moved towards the big black book. 'But let's not concern ourselves with that. There was a row, you said?'

Potter shifted from one buttock to the other. 'It began with one of these hippies throwing beer over the landlord.'

'And what did you do that was so helpful?'

Potter sighed. 'I flung my own beer over the hippy.'

'Ah,' said Grue.

'He'd jostled me when he came to order more beer. Then I heard him shout something about horse-piss and there was a splash, and when I turned the landlord was standing there dripping and the hippy was laughing his head off, so I flung my own beer at him.'

11

Grue considered the pudgy little figure with interest and what might have been approval. 'And then?'

'Next thing I knew I was down on the floor trying to keep a bar stool between my stomach and the hippy's boot. There was a lot of shouting and stamping of feet and the girl was shrieking. When I got up they were throwing the last of the hippies out.'

'A breach of the peace, Mr Potter?'

'Off the record, you said. Anyway, where were your coppers when they might have been of some use? The copper warming pans were more useful. They look better too, more decorative than your coppers, certainly more decorative than that one with the rabbits.'

'Rabbits?'

'Yes, rabbits. The one in plain clothes who smelled of sheep.'

Grue stared. 'Rabbits? Sheep?'

'And wire snares round his neck. I might have put that in my letter to the Chief Constable.'

'You could hardly have apologised for the way the constables were dressed or how they smelled.' Grue made a note. 'But go on with your story.'

'It wasn't much that I had done but the locals made a lot of it. So since I was well in with them I asked if they knew of a cottage for sale. I'd been looking for one, you see, and agents only send you to clapped-out ruins with astronomic prices. The landlord took me to the window and pointed across the street. "There," he said, and I'd get it cheap. Nobody in the village wanted it. Not enough room for a washing machine or a fridge. A good enough little house, though, and I'd get the furniture as well, for the previous owner had died in Africa and left no heirs. I went to the solicitor who was the agent and had a look at it, and it was just what I wanted, so I bought it right away. That's it then. Can I go now?'

'What furniture was there?'

'Only a bed and a gas cooker. The lawyer likely took the rest. He'll have my money too, I expect. He's pretty sharp, they say; but people always do say that about lawyers, don't they. It's a good bed, though, a double bed. The previous owner had unscrewed it and squeezed it into a diamond shape to get it up the stairs and it'll never be got down again.' Potter yawned. 'I really must be going.'

'Not quite yet, Mr Potter. I want to know what happened when you met Boyle down by the canal. Tell me what he said.'

Potter got up and stretched. 'All right, but I'm going to walk about a bit.'

It was a hot day, a Sunday. Potter had gone for a stroll after lunch. It was very peaceful by the canal, only the sound of bursting broom pods disturbed the silence. He went on along the towpath till he came to the bridge that carries the canal across a stream and stopped there to lean over and look down at the water, the willow branches and the weeds trailing in the current. In the shadow of the bridge there was a long shape that attracted his attention. It was motionless in the current and he leaned over farther to see how it could be held there. And then he saw that it did have motion, an incessant flicker at its sides. A hand gripped his arm and a voice spoke beside him. 'It's a pike.'

Potter looked round, startled, looked into flat brown eyes. 'You've bought Brown's house,' the man said.

He was flabby and his eyes were like a bullock's. Potter twisted his arm away and looked back down into the stream. 'The shark of the rivers.' The hand dropped on to Potter's arm again. 'Oh, the perils that lurk in the waters of life!' The hand slid along Potter's arm. 'The dreary document, it's mine.'

Potter lifted off the hand as one would any unpleasant thing. 'I don't know what you're talking about.'

'Papers. The dreary document.'

'You'd better ask the lawyer,' Potter said.

'Tahag,' the man said, just that single word, 'Tahag', and it brought Potter's head round sharply. The flat brown eyes looked into his and in them something stirred, as things stir from the bottom of a stagnant pool. 'You will give me the papers,' the man said, and there might have been menace in the words but that his north-country accent recalled radio comedians. 'Remember the perils that lurk in the waters of life!' and he thrust a piece of paper into Potter's hand.

Without another word Potter left him. He looked back once. The man was shambling off along the towpath with the ungainly movements of a bullock. His trousers didn't fit.

'What was on the paper?' Grue asked.

'His name, Roger Boyle. And a telephone number. I threw it in the canal.'

'That word he used, Tahag, it had some meaning for you?'

'Yes, it did.' Potter sat down. 'It's a place in Egypt. Brown wrote a story about it. That's the dreary document Boyle spoke of. It's a story about a man called Dreerie.' Potter spelled it. 'I have it in my office, took it there to read it over again but never got around to it.'

'You didn't mention this before.'

'It didn't seem important. I found it in the lavatory. You can have it if you wish, though I don't see it as being of any use to you. Goodness knows why Boyle made such a fuss about it.'

'That word, Tahag, he seems to have used it to startle you

14

into an admission that you had read the story. It didn't occur to you that he really was its owner?'

'Perhaps he was, but I wasn't going to hand it over to him just on his say-so. Anyway there's nothing to it. Except . . .'

'Except what?'

'Oh, nothing. There's nothing to it. You can read it for yourself.' Potter got to his feet. 'I'm going now. You said you would have me taken to the University. I'll give the story to the driver.'

'Very well, Mr Potter. You have been patient.' Grue considered Potter thoughtfully for a moment or two. 'The car will take you to your office, and home afterwards if you don't keep it waiting too long. But I must have that story. It could have been for that story that Boyle broke into your house, and for that story he was murdered.'

Potter cancelled his classes for the day and gave the story to the driver. 'Home, James,' he instructed. The driver wasn't one of the snoopers in the lane but it was nice to be ordering the fuzz about.

Faces peered curiously from behind curtains as the police car drew up at Potter's door. The landlord came over from the pub. 'You'll find the place in decent order. My wife's been in with her vacuum cleaner, got in through the broken window. Nobody will bother you – we'll hear the story soon enough.'

Potter's cottage, one of a row built to house the supervisors of the navvies when the canal was dug, was a compact little house, two up, two down, the front door opening on to the living room, the back door leading from the kitchen to the garden. Just outside the back door was a brick structure which housed a lavatory, and it was there that Potter had found the Dreerie story. A wooden box held a supply of newspaper, collected presumably by the previous owner for his use. During a prolonged session Potter had been reading through some of these old papers when he came across a bundle of handwritten sheets. With them was a letter, a note rather:

I found the story and the other papers exactly where you said they would be. What it lacks, I think, is feminine interest. It won't do to leave women out now. By the last decade of this century every book will be written by a woman. This is written in haste. My appointment to the Examining Board has been confirmed and I am buying a house in Bath. Write to me at 13 Loofah Crescent.

It was addressed to 'Mr Brown' and signed 'Janet Pring'. Potter neglected to give this letter to the police with the story.

'"O Hooghie, Hooghie, Hooghie!"' read the Chief Constable. 'What's that?'

'It's a farm in Scotland, sir.'

'And you want me to read this thing?'

'You'll see why shortly, sir. But consider its importance in the case. This story has been the cause of burglary and murder and it is the only clue we've got.'

The Chief Constable riffled through the pile of sheets. 'Oh very well.' Reluctantly he began to read.

Part 2

All for the Best

O Hooghie, Hooghie, Hooghie! All night long the howlet cried, a weird to be dreed, Dreerie no more Dreerie of Hooghie. Far across the sea to Australia I was bound – there was no money.

From my window I could see the wheelmarks on the gravel where the hearse had turned before that slow procession up the hill past pensive cows and sheep bleating mournful farewell to their kindly master. Another now would send them to the butcher.

Black coats and black umbrellas, red faces over unaccustomed collars, hollow thump of clay on wood.

When I went downstairs Mr Macrabbit was already at his breakfast. Every summer he came to pass his holiday in our house since his call from the village kirk to a busier pulpit in the city, him and his three unmarried sisters, and he was come again to pay his last respects. He gripped my arm. I wept. 'The Ministry,' he said, 'the Ministry of the Kirk. You have been brought up in godly ways and it's a fair living, John.' He lifted up his eyes to the ceiling where the hams were hanging on their hooks.

In my mind's eye I saw black-robed figures in their pulpits, masterful, respected. 'But how could that be, Mr Macrabbit?'

Jean, the maid, put down his second plate of bacon

and eggs. 'Bursaries,' he said, 'there's bursaries'll see you through, you'll get through university with bursaries.'

'Who's he?'

'Not he, it's what, or how much, rather. Bursaries is money left by godly folk to see young men into the Ministry of the Kirk. You've only two more terms at the Garbage School until you get your certificates. The fees are paid and bursaries'll see you through university.'

I'd thought of university as a place where things were bought and sold like at the cattle market in our county town. And Ministers, I supposed they just happened, like thunderstorms, or when the brodie produced her litter of wee pigs. There was a lot I didn't understand and would have asked him about, but he was deep in calculation. 'The Carnegie Trust, of course. I canna mind a' the rest but the Scowler Fund is forty pund, the Glaur's another forty. Wi' Donnart and Glaikit, twa hunner I make it . . . Oh, John, I've written poetry afore now. I get carried away when I think on bonny things!'

Poetry! Like Robert Burns himself! 'All that money, Mr Macrabbit!'

'Aye, and mair besides. There's the McClang Bursary for Descendants of Honest Blacksmiths and a grant for Teetotallers of the Original Secession. Oh aye, and the Fflewzay Fund for Decayed Gentlewomen and' – he gripped my arm excitedly – 'the Bonny Clyde Bequest. That's best of all! It's money from American banks!' He told of men toiling in mines and steelworks, on railways and on ships to get me into the Ministry. He pictured happy faces in steam and smoke and kindly employers who made this labour possible. With arms held high he spoke of banks and how readily they gave out money. 'Strange are the ways of Providence,' he mused. 'Now go and feed the hens.'

So it was with new hope that I went back to George Garbage's School for my last two terms. A good way out of a bad job, the family thought. Uncle Hector had some pin-striped breeks that no longer fitted and I could wear for preaching in. And I could pass my holidays at Girnie, cutting kale and hoeing turnips. An extra hand was useful too at the harvest and the lifting of the tatties.

Mr Macrabbit went back to the city to look up bursaries, with a pair of vases from our sideboard that he took for sentiment's sake and a few hens that Jean had plucked for him. He liked well a hen did Mr Macrabbit.

I never saw Hooghie again. Memories remained though, the most vivid of a day of storm, and a cart rumbling down the slope of the Dominie's Field, harness clinking and creaking with the heaves and plunges of the horse. The hind and me were wrapped in tatty sacks against the driving rain. The hind complained of long, long hours and the money a' tae the Big Hoose. And I have minded since how the steward used to count out wages on our back kitchen table, little piles of shilling pieces.

Through the last days of school and early days of university those turnips rattled round my head, though socialism is what I thought they were. It was a time of loss, betrayal and defeat in the wider world, and all this stirred resentment in me so that I was ready to strike back. There is a madness that comes upon us Scots at times, the wild madness of the Highland blood that stirs us from our sober Lowland ways. The madness came upon me in the last week of school outside the headmaster's study.

I had been passing that door for seven years but now I saw it as for the first time, the copper plate with his name and all the rest, symbol of pride and privilege. I had a vision then, a vision like yon man had on the road to Casablanca. Or was it Samarkand? I'd take that copper plate.

Seven years had Jacob laboured. What for I couldna mind, but he got his reward and I'd have mine. Something ere the end, some work of noble note might yet be done. The copper plate would do. Screws – I'd need a screwdriver. And something to break in with. I found it in an empty crate outside the chemistry laboratory, a crowbar. I dropped it through a window into bushes down below.

That very night I lay in the dormitory waiting for all the restless noise to cease. When at last they were all asleep I put on my clothes and eased the window up. There was a drainpipe to hold on to and ivy to give footholds. In the garden nothing stirred; the streets were empty all the way to the great gates. Where they joined the wall I climbed over.

Goal posts loomed like gibbets. The playing fields were deserted, no shivering victims forced to run about with cries of false enthusiasm for teams called A and B, thrown arbitrarily together and into strife. On ground as muddy in life's sterner struggle I have found things much the same. Rows of windows looked blackly out. I tried a side door and it opened. There was luck – no need for crowbar and sounds of splintering wood. I went directly to the headmaster's door.

The screws came out easily. The copper plate was in my hands. It did not seem enough. The door opened when I turned the handle. Behind the great desk was a tall shape. It was ... it was only his chair, his high-backed chair. I moved along the side of the desk, one hand on it for guidance, and sat down on the chair.

In a few minutes there I learned more of worth than

all they'd taught through seven long years. It matters where you sit in life. From one chair you give orders. In another you receive them – if you're offered any seat at all. Beside the white rectangle that was the blotting pad there was another white rectangle. A letter, stamped, unopened. I stuffed it down inside my shirt and went. I ran and the corridor creaked and rattled. Somewhere a clock was striking. The gates seemed higher. I hurried along the darker sides of the streets. Into the garden. Up the pipe, plate clanking, foot slipping on the ivy. Head in at the window. Nothing, not a sound.

I must have slept but it seemed no time till the morning light. I took the letter to the lavatory. A foreign stamp – it would do for my collection – and another envelope inside, 'To be opened in the event of my falling in action'. I read the letter that was with it. It had a printed heading – 'The Garngad Highlanders'. I understood most of what it said, though not it all.

'My regiment!' The Chief Constable was astounded. 'That's my regiment!'

'You see now why I want you to read the story, sir.'

The Chief Constable took up another sheet. His swizzle-stick began to beat the air.

Sir,

Amongst the effects of the late Frederick Lillie was found the enclosed envelope. The Lieutenant has been listed as Fallen in Action, both for the honour of the Regiment and because it does not depart too far from the truth, but I owe it to your responsible office to inform you that the Lieutenant expired from a number of loathsome diseases contracted by his lodgement in a garbage bin.

To state the matter briefly. The Commander of the Guard on the Women's Army Compound having heard shrieks disturb the night, he instituted a search whereby Lieutenant Lillie was discovered hiding in a garbage bin. I regret to say that he was improperly dressed.

A Court of Enquiry, subsequently assembled, established to its satisfaction that the Lieutenant had been in bed with one of the female personnel, that he had withdrawn to seek natural relief, and that on his return to the dormitory he had introduced himself into the wrong bed. Both of the female personnel were outraged.

The Lieutenant's demise from the above-mentioned diseases is consistent with his concealment in the above-mentioned garbage-bin and no blame is attached to either of the female personnel.

> I have the honour to be, Sir,
> Your obedient servant,
> Angus Neil ban Gaiters-Gooch
> (Captain/Adjutant)

I hurriedly opened the smaller envelope. The letter in it was much more interesting,

Dear Headmaster,

Whilst on shore leave at Gibraltar, and in the confusion that ensued when the Military Police entered a hostelry where I was being entertained, I acquired a suitcase of which the contents proved to be of considerable value. Loot, perchance, from the Spanish Civil

War, for the case bore the label of Spanish Railways in Seville.

Our convoy proceeded to Port Said, whence we were moved directly to the garrison of Tahag. I have concealed the treasure in St Andrew's Church, of which I am Session Clerk. Its hiding place will be revealed by the Beadle, Ali Mooman Effendi, on presentation of agreed symbols – an Old Garbagean tie and the Best Boy of the Year Trophy. Ali, being illiterate, is entirely to be trusted. He will always be found at the church for his salary is to be paid in perpetuity from regimental funds.

Should I fall in action it is my desire that proceeds from the treasure shall be devoted to construction of a Fred Lillie Cricket Pavilion for the old school. Was not George Garbage's original foundation from like sources?

Farewell dear Headmaster. *Sur kabacha*! I have not forgotten the old school's motto. And you will not have forgotten your Best Boy, Fred.

'This is outrageous!' The Chief Constable slammed the paper down.

'Quite so, sir. But did you know these officers, Lieutenant Lillie and Captain Gaiters-Gooch?'

'Lillie, no. But I knew Angus Gaiters-Gooch, Major then.' For a few moments the Chief Constable was lost in memories. 'Angus Gaiters-Gooch. I wouldn't want Angus to read this stuff.'

'So the letter is not genuine, sir?'

'Good God, no! Angus was a fine officer.'

'But at least we have established something in the story that is not fiction, even if it's just a name. You must read the rest, sir.'

The Chief Constable hesitated. 'Angus was always a stick-
ler on the subject of proper dress ... but no, it can't be
genuine ... What's a beadle? Sort of verger, isn't it?'

'That's what they're called in Scotland, sir, and a session
clerk is a churchwarden, more or less.'

The Chief Constable grunted and took up another sheet.

I whistled and someone beat on the lavatory door.
Here was destiny! A treasure that no one else could
know of! The Best Boy Trophy – it was in the headmaster's office. I had seen it there. It was a wooden
thing, carved by some art teacher into the shape of a
melting ice-cream cone. It was awarded every year to
the school's greatest creep. Dare I go back for it?

Brooding on the treasure and on the Trophy, I had
all but forgotten the copper plate and it was absent-
mindedly that I showed it to another of the boarders.
He betrayed me. He went and told. Play-up-for-the-old-
school! Let him remain nameless in perfidy!

Named by the nameless, summoned to the nameless
door, I passed through it to judgment and retribution.

The headmaster stood at the window, back turned
on the rise and fall of the leather tawse. Duty done,
the janitor departed. And still the headmaster's back
was turned. I snatched the Trophy and stuffed it down
one leg as I pulled my trousers up.

So it was not without honour that I limped away
from George Garbage's School. Seven years had Jacob
laboured. He probably learned more than I did but
mine could be the greater reward.

Through that long summer I hoed and howked at
Girnie and turnips rattled in my head. They rattled still

24

in early days of student poverty. Unerring was the finger of Karl Marx when he put it upon capital. Income is what you need to live on, and you don't need much for that. But capital is shoes without holes and a warm coat.

Then the bursaries started to come in and the change was revolutionary. In ones and twos they came – Scowler, McClang and Glaur, Donnart and Glaikit, the Original Secession, Fflewzay. My landlady would put the letters on the mantelpiece, where I found them when I came in from classes. It was near the end of term when Bonny Clyde burst in.

'Did you get your letter?' asked Miss Taik when I went through for my tea.

I went to look again, stepping over Willie's out-stretched legs. 'No letter here, Miss Taik.'

'On the mantelpiece.' Busy with her potato pie.

Willie, the medical student who shared the room with me, was deep in a text-book, puffing smoke with irritating pops. It was the one with the indecent pictures. 'I don't see it, Miss Taik,' I called.

She came to look herself. Willie pop-pop-popped and moved his legs and went on popping. 'A big white envelope it was. From America. Where's it gone?' Plucking at empty air along the mantelpiece. 'Maybe it fell. What's this?' Knocking the charred end from paper in the fireplace. 'It's your letter, Mr Dreerie! That's terrible! Mr McLemon's gone and used it for his pipe!'

From his envelope of smoke Willie reached out a hand. 'Errors can be made. These things happen. Let's have it opened up.' With the scalpel he used for cleaning his pipe he made a swift incision, flexed his fingers and inserted two. 'Ha! What have we here? A cheque! A fine, bouncing . . . well anyway a cheque! A

25

little singed, a crease or two. Your iron, Miss Taik, to smooth it out?'

It was for four hundred dollars! What would that be in real money? Near enough two hundred pounds, they thought.

From that day the turnips ceased to rattle. I left them to Marx, who is as indigestible. Full marks to Marx though – half Marx as it turned out – who showed the way to Egypt. But that was potatoes. And cups of tea.

The city is inhabited by ladies of middling years with glasses and sore feet, and their opinion of everything that happens is 'That's terrible!' but 'tearable' is the way they say it. And that is how my story will be judged if I do not abbreviate this next section.

Two pairs of glasses swivelled from the rucksack and were brought to bear on Willie. 'That's terrible!' The ladies had been clawing down from the platform of the tram, sore feet feeling for the next step, when Willie, reversing the known order of things, had shoved up past them a rucksack full of porridge oats and tins of beans. I pulled it into greater safety as the tram clanged into motion and left them behind. I was off to the Highlands.

Willie had come up with the notion of youth hostelling as a better way of passing holidays than cutting kale at Girnie. It was easy to hitch-hike, he said. All you needed to do was wave your thumb with confidence and smile. That was the important thing, to smile. And what was so funny about his car breaking down, a driver asked the first time I tried it. But that first night I got to Kirriemuir. It was dark by then, and the streets deserted but for a man poking at the pillar box. All he said was 'Fower and twunty, fower and twunty' when I asked the way.

I found a wayside shelter with a bench, and slept there. In the early light of the next morning I walked on in the direction of Cortachy, to which a broken sign had pointed. I was hungry and could fine have lightened my pack of some porridge oats or a tin of beans had there been any way of cooking. I went on up the glen till the road ended, and on a track, then, through the birchwoods and on to the open moor where the whaups were crying, and never a sign of Cortachy.

'A black backit paitrick flew ower the kirk at Cortachy.' It was a tongue-twister I had learned in childhood and I said it over and over as I climbed up to the crest, hoping that the paitrick would do its droppings on the whole village and all its inhabitants.

Far down on the other side of the pass there was a castle, the only building I could see anywhere. I called out when I reached the door but nobody came, and since I found no bell or knocker, I just walked in. Surely they would give me a glass of milk or a bowl of porridge.

And then there was a burst of singing, the sound of many voices from a room in front of me. I opened the door. Along the sides of two long tables stood a fair-sized company, their mouths opening and shutting like animated pillar-box slots.

> Goodness ha-and me-hercy ha-all my li-hife
> Shall su-hurely fo-hollow me-he . . .

There were tureens of steaming soup upon the tables and it was a slow, slow tune. Not *Crimond*, nor *Wiltshire*. It was *The Red Flag*. But they were done at last and I found a place and was reaching for a ladle as my pack

27

slipped to the floor. Nobody said anything and I had more soup. Then came plates of pie and I had two helpings of it. Someone was reading from a book and I mumbled something to my neighbour.

'Wheesht!' he said. 'Engles.'

The reading was about factories in Manchester. Ah, there *was* butter! But what had factories in Manchester to do with geometry?

I had noticed that my neighbour had not been eating. 'I hope, sir, it was not your pie I ate,' I said to him when the reading stopped. I have been well brought up.

'I don't eat pie.' *Eh don't eat peh* – he must be from the city and might be sympathetic to a hungry student.

'I just walked in, you see. I'm an intruder.'

'You don't say. I'm an Anthropososogist myself. That's why I don't eat pie. We're very ecumenical here.'

'I was hungry. I'd eaten nothing since yesterday.'

'That's terrible! But have you been integrated?'

'What's that, sir? Integrated? I belong to the Youth Hostels.'

'Don't use that word to me!'

'But you used it yourself, sir.'

'There are no sirs in this dichotomy. Call me comrade!'

'What's a dichotomy, sir . . . comrade?'

'A dichotomy is a cleavage. We have embraced a cleavage. Christian Communism is our dichotomy. Ah, roly-poly!'

As we ate our pudding he told me of the Dichotomy. It was well endowed and all who were integrated could stay there free of charge.

I was integrated after lunch. All I had to do was

promise to wear a workman's shirt on Sundays and dungarees at Easter and at Christmas.

'Arise ye starvelings from your slumbers!' There was a strong smell of bacon frying and it seemed long since last night's mutton chops. 'Arise ye wretched of the earth!' What a slow tune is *Onward Christian Soldiers*, but at last it dragged to an end. '*The Internationale* unites the human race.' And still breakfast didn't come. The same reader was reading.

'Kropotkin,' said the Anthropososogist. No cereal appeared. The same reader was reading. You'll have heard him on the BBC. Introduces the religious programmes and soothing music.

At last the reader slipped to a stop and everybody said 'Amen'. And breakfast came. I had three helpings.

I owe two things to the Dichotomy. I discovered how to get to Egypt, but that was on the way back to the city. Perhaps more important, I gained knowledge which gave me power to summon Professor Hubble to my aid. It may have been the Devil himself who guided me.

After breakfast I climbed the tower of the castle for a view of the surrounding countryside. On a windswept platform there was a figure all in black brooding on the battlements. He seized me by the arm and whirled the other hand about. 'All these are mine!' he cried. He pointed South. 'King Edward!' He drew me to the North where the wind brought tears to my eyes. 'Arran Banner!' But proud Edward's power had been brought low at Bannockburn, the banners of Arran no longer marched against him! Yet again the man in black whirled round and pointed East, where the sun shone in splendour. 'Golden Wonder! Majestic!' And finally he led me to the West where shadows lay upon the mountains. 'Eclipse,' he muttered sadly. 'Lucky if they get Grade C.'

Scottish seed potatoes are the envy of less favoured lands, their purity preserved by roguers. The roguer is able to tell a hundred different types of potato at a glance and it is his office to extirpate the wrong ones. The man in black was a roguer, and there on the tower he named names that would grace any robust rose and stand in Scotland's proud story with battles and clans and brands of whisky. I determined that I would come to know them and be a roguer too, for the profession is well paid.

I have often wondered at the strange turns of fate that took me to Tahag. It was as in some ancient Celtic rune, some prophecy of Thomas Rhymer, who lies waiting in the Eildon Hills. Named by the nameless, summoned to the nameless door. And then the numbers. Seven, always seven, but for the number whispered to me in Kirriemuir. Put down 7 twice and 24. Subtract one from the other and you have 17. Two more sevens is 14 and add another 7 and you have 7724147. The weird was dreed.

The Anthropososogist gave me a lift back to the city, where he had a sweetie shop and wrote stories for the weekly magazines. On the way he told of the moral dangers which confront our troops in Egypt: women and wine and wickedness of other sorts. Only by a constant supply of tea can their virtue be preserved, he said, and to this task his All-square Circle was committed in their canteens for the troops. Our national Kirk was in on it too and labourers were needed in the teeyard.

The car broke down in the suburbs of the city. 'That's terrible!' cried the Anthropososogist. 'My wife and our three wee dichotomies will be waiting and I must get in my story before the office shuts!'

'I'll take it,' I said, 'and phone your wife.' There was a tram waiting just along the road.

I got my name in for a course of roguing right away and I saw the canteens people too. I never saw that castle again. I can't even remember what it was called. And the Anthropososogist, I never saw him again either.

A shriek girned round the walls. Miss Taik had found our dirty boots. She'd still to see the bathroom.

'The plumber got away with worse.' I squeezed a rag into the bucket resentfully.

'That's how trades differ from professions,' brooded Willie, leaning on the mop. 'Tradesmen learn the things that matter. In colleges they only stuff your head with useless knowledge.'

Willie and I had qualified as roguers and now faced the practical problems of the profession. We solved the one of muddy boots by sleeping in a bothy. Straw on a wooden platform made our beds. We stewed our suppers in an iron cauldron suspended on a chain. The thoughts of vagrant Irish labourers were recorded on the walls.

We might still have made something of it that summer had not Willie seen every potato as a patient with ailments to diagnose or to invent. He decimated whole rows with ruthless surgery or lingered half a day over a

31

single plant to perfect his bedside manner. Our progress was spasmodic and we finally got bogged down in wet Gladstones in Midlothian.

The following summer Willie was gone, failed Second Profs, and peeling potatoes in the Army Medical Corps. Davie, the partner I found to succeed him, was not much to look at, thin as a rake and stooped as if aye looking for a sixpence, but he had a way with the farmers and the potato merchants.

I was now half way through for my degree in the Obscure Languages and, though it was unlikely that I would be spending another three years there, I thought it wise to have a look round the College of Divinity. I am of a diffident character and like to look the ground over when a new venture is to be undertaken.

I slipped past the janitor one night when his back was turned, and had the place to myself, for the college is not residential. The most important thing I found was a way of private access. Some work had been being done on the fireplace in the dining room and they'd gone off leaving it unfinished. There was a hole through to a courtyard at the back and it was separated from the street only by an iron railing. I found a gallery that was airy, yet would be warmed up by the sun at weekends, and there Davie and I settled for the summer. There were plush benches to sleep on and we got in and out easily, though Davie tore his breeks once when he came back drunk.

We rogued there for two summers and then Davie joined the army and got himself killed. It was only then that I learned he was cousin's son to our old Laird at Hooghie. Och Davie, he was aye borrowing money.

I went roguing one more summer, the summer after they gave me my degree. It was eerie in the college alone at night and I was feared for ghosts. It is a rambling old place with long galleries and winding staircases and gloomy halls. One night I was awakened and lay listening. There was a thud and three more thuds, from somewhere up above. There was light on the walls of the staircases. Another thud. I got up and crept along and fearfully looked up. The light flickered, making shadows that swayed and wavered. I went up step by step. The light was coming from the gallery where the oldest books were kept, books on witchcraft were there too. There was a rustling noise that might have been a snake. I looked through the open door.

In the light of a guttering candle shone the bald head of Professor Hubble. He was edging brown paper under a pile of books bound in calfskin. The light glittered too on rimless glasses across the table. The Professor bound the pile with string and looked expectantly at the other, one hand upon the parcel. The rimless glasses flashed as the other bent over a wallet and counted out money. I saw that he had a turtle chin. He passed the money over and the Professor counted, licking a finger after every note.

It was dusty up there and I sneezed, so I slipped back and ran to hide. But I had heard enough to tell me that the Professor's accomplice was an American and, for his part, Professor Hubble used language that was not obscure.

Professor Hubble holds the University's chair in Obscure Languages, so that it was under him that I had studied, but he was also the Right Reverend Recognizant of Rectitude and Provisor of Proper Persons for the Pulpits of the Kirk. It was in this ecclesiastical capacity that he summoned me to his office. There is an examination in Bible Knowledge for entrants to the Faculty of Divinity and it seemed that I had failed, though I had forgotten that I ever sat it.

He looked up furtively from sheets of paper that I recognised to be my answers to the test. He cackled. 'Sodom and Gomorrah were man and wife! He, he! And Hiddekel was buried treasure? "hid shekels" you have it here. It winna dae, Dreerie, it winna dae. Hooever . . . ye hae a guid degree. Honours in the Obscure Languages with distinction in Aramaic, Armenian and Esperanto.' He pursed his lips. 'Noo I am wulling to stretch your mark by the one per cent you need if . . .' He scratched his nose. 'If you will undertake to study your Bible releegiously.'

I groaned and closed my eyes and rocked back and forwards and droned like an Episcopalian.

> Oh I hae dreamed a dreary dream
> Ayont the Isle o' Skye . . .

I opened wide my eyes. 'Strange dreams, Professor, I have had strange dreams.'

'Whit dreams is this?'

'Dreams about beds and books, Professor. I made my bed in the college through the summer and dreamed of books. Was it not the great Alexander White who urged his students to sell their beds and buy books? Or was it the other way about? And I dreamed of Pharaoh and Jacob and of fat years and of lean years and now I am off to Egypt and I'm needing more than one per cent.'

'Egypt? Egypt? How's that?'

'I am going to do my bit for King and country. I'm going to make tea for the troops.'

'Whit for are they needin' you tae make their tea?'

'It's not the tea that's needed, it's canteens, and so

tea has to be made in them and I'm to do it. The canteens people were impressed when I told them that all my ancestors fell in the Battle of Tel-el-Kebir, so they're sending me to Tahag, which is not far off.'

'Ye don't say!'

'So I'll be needing money. There's a Fiddell Fellowship in Coptic, three hundred pounds, I think, and isn't there something for Waddells in the Holy Land?'

Of my journey to Egypt little need be said. England is best crossed by night and the sea is not much more remarkable. But its movement is in all our songs of exile and I thought on all I'd lost as the ship moved out into the great waters. And then there came to me the memory of the *Old Hundredth* as they used to sing it in our village kirk, its grandeur and assurance. In my hand I held my bible – what for I cannot say, unless it was some pledge I'd made to Professor Hubble. I flung it wildly upwards. It fluttered for a moment, white against the sky, then fell down into the ship's wake where the cold light of the moon mingled with the gold of the passing day. It is the only religious experience I ever had.

'Grue, I have read enough of this.'

'Where have you got to, sir?' Grue turned the sheet that the Chief Constable had dropped. 'You're just coming to the interesting bit where he finds the treasure.'

'But there's nothing in it that could be true. It's just nonsense!'

Grue pushed aside the pages that his Chief had read. 'The rest is different. There's a character called Boyle in it and there are significant resemblances to what we know of our murdered Boyle. You must read it, sir. There are further references to your regiment.'

'I suppose I might as well finish it now I've got this far.' Grimly the Chief Constable took up the next sheet.

This should not be read by those who desire to take degrees in Psychology, Performing Arts or Media Studies.

I stepped off the gangway on to the soil of Egypt. Perhaps I was on the very spot where Lillie had landed with his suitcase full of treasure.

There was no sign of the officer who had come to take me to Tahag. He had appeared when I was trying to attract the attention of the purser. 'What could the purser do about your case? One Egyptian disappearing through a port-hole would look like any other. Bring the rest of what you've got.' He waved a little leather stick.

All around me were shouting mouths and squinting eyes and a sickly smell of breath. Hands waved and plucked. My one remaining case was torn away. I cried out in Arabic and the seething mass became an interested audience. As I explained myself, the audience became a purposeful progression that pushed and pulled me through the dock gates to a yellow bus. 'Make way,' they cried, 'make way for the effendi who speaks our tongue!'

From every window of the bus ferocious faces glared out at the hubbub. They wore peaked caps such as you can see in photographs of atrocious Japanese. One jerked his chin. 'You the canteen wallah? Where's Paddy?'

'There was an officer who said he would meet me at

the foot of the gangway but he's disappeared and so has all my luggage.'

'Oh get in.'

Gentle Egyptian hands lifted me aboard. I found a seat at the back and all the faces turned and glared. Could they be commandos? 'Paddy' seemed a disrespectful way to speak of an officer but perhaps it was like that in the commandos. And then I saw that they wore RAF badges. Probably there wasn't much time for courtesies in the RAF with all that flying about they had to do.

The officer got in. 'Hello Paddy!' they all cried. 'What are we waiting for?'

He started counting, pointing with his little leather stick. But past him pushed Egyptians carrying suitcases. They dropped the cases at my seat. Two of them were mine. After an exchange of courtesies they shuffled back along the bus uttering ululations. At the door one waved a little leather stick.

The bus moved off, swerving out between donkeys and camels and lorries loading and unloading. The officer was looking out over the driver's shoulder and giving him directions. We passed through the town and out into the desert. And then a very strange thing happened. The airmen took off their peaked caps and all ferocity was wiped away, gone as though it had never been. The faces now were gentle, with that simple amiable expression you see on the faces of the inhabitants of remote villages where everyone is related to one another. They brought out cardboard boxes and began to eat.

The officer gave the driver some final instructions and then scrambled along the passage to where I was sitting. 'That's my seat!'

I moved to the one beside and he climbed over to sit by the window. He was restless, sometimes half rising in his seat, muttering to himself. His hand was on a revolver at his belt. Once he caught my eye and gave me a grim smile. 'Watch for El Ballah.'

On both sides of the road the sand stretched evenly away to the horizon. There was no place from which attack might come. No Bedouin on racing camels brandishing spears and rifles. In the distance appeared white-washed buildings. A fort? The officer regarded them intently. A road junction flashed past. A sign-board said *El Ballah. British Military Hospital.*

The officer relaxed though his hand was never far from the revolver at his belt. He began to tell me of Tahag. 'Things,' he muttered, 'things go on there that could tilt the whole world balance of power.' He glanced over his shoulder to where there was an armed guard with a gun more or less firmly under his feet and a bottle of beer upended in his mouth. 'Security is tight.'

The garrison was mixed, he told me, the cream of both the army and the RAF. The army was guarding vast stores of equipment accumulated through the years of war. The RAF were a mysterious lot, linguists and experts in electronics who listened in to conversations in Moscow and overheard footfalls in Tel Aviv. There were parts of the camp so secret that no-one had ever entered them.

We came to another canal, which the officer told me was the Sweetwater. Women all in black were washing clothes and drawing up water in clay pots. People squatted with their backs to the canal and their robes pulled up. On the other side of the road peasants poked at the soil. Donkeys brayed and ambled round in circles. A child lay at the roadside, covered in dirt.

'Just like the Bible,' said the officer, and made a careful note.

The road rose away from the canal, back into the desert. The airmen were singing:

> This is my story, this is my song . . .

'Fine lads,' said the officer. 'They're National Servicemen. It's a privilege to serve with them.' The singing swelled in volume. 'The lads do like a rousing hymn,' said the officer. 'We must be getting near Tahag.'

A forest of radio masts bristled in the distance. Great sheds appeared, row upon row, stretching in every direction. The bus halted at a barrier. The airmen put on their peaked caps and glared ferociously as it lifted. We rolled into the camp and the airmen sang:

> This is my story, this is my song,
> I've been in the Air Force
> Too fuckin' long . . .

'Don't suppose I'll be seeing much of you,' said the officer as we got off the bus. 'Great things are happening, you know.' He gave me a significant nod. 'All the time we are in conference. But maybe you could come on one of our moral leadership courses. The one we've been on in Port Said was particularly inspiring. Padre Pew Jones was splendid on the dual-purpose penis. Sex, you know, that's the thing. Yes, you must come on one of these.'

The canteen was a pleasant hut in which two Egyptians made tea and sandwiches and I had a room to sleep in. I unpacked only what I needed immediately, and without further delay asked to be directed to St Andrew's Church. Nobody had ever heard of it. There wasn't one. There was a garrison church for the English, and the Catholics had theirs, but there wasn't any St Andrew's.

There had to be! There must be one! There wasn't. There were seven.

They told me I should enquire at Garrison Headquarters, and that was easily found for there were signposts everywhere pointing to it. The first door I opened was marked 'BRIG' and a red-faced man shouted at me rudely. There were some airmen painting stones outside, quite pretty really, though they might have used some other colours as well as white. They thought that would be a good idea too and asked that I should mention it in the orderly room, where they answered all enquiries.

I don't know how it got its name. The orderly room was full of trestle tables all covered with sheets of paper and the only one there was a flabby man with a uniform that didn't fit him. However, he was smart enough in getting to his feet and saluting. The uniform jacket I wore must have impressed him with the teacups it had on the epaulettes.

'On me track, sir,' he said. 'The rest are at their NAAFI break.'

There was something familiar about him. Where could I have seen him before?

He didn't know anything about St Andrew's Church, so I told him to carry on and I would wait. There were a lot of rubber stamps on one table, so I tried them out on some of the paper I found there. It passed the time until three other airmen came and a corporal. They didn't know anything about St Andrew's Church but they gave me a card that listed fifteen functionaries I would have to see and have it initialled by them all.

'The Binbrook System,' said the corporal. 'It gives everybody something to do.'

The first functionary was SLOP and I was being given directions how to find him when a sergeant bustled in. 'What's this then, what's this? You won't find SLOP there now. He's gone to Ish. Who's next? God save us all, there's Boyle. I thought you were transferred to GOP? What's that you're on?'

'Me track,' said the airman, whom I had found alone when I came in. 'It was me brother that was sent to GOP. And now he's been demobbed and took some of me tracks with him.'

'Could we send Boyle off with this fellow, Sarge? He's looking for a church.'

'Well, put all the churches on the Binbrook Card and put the mosque on too. Let's get things moving!'

'It's a St Andrew's Church he wants, but there isn't one.'

'There will be if I put it on the card. Bring a map and find somewhere for him to go.'

They spread a map out and suddenly a finger stabbed.

'Look, there it is!'

But almost at the same time another finger stabbed. 'No, there!' And other alert fingers were stabbing at the map 'There! There! There!'

All seven were right. There were seven St Andrew's churches!

All of them were outside the perimeter of the present camp. How could I get to any of them and which was Lillie's? There were roads marked to each one but they would have disappeared under drifting sand. I

41

could borrow the map, though, and they would send LAC Boyle, their expert in religion, to help find the churches. They rolled up the map and put it in the hand of the airman I had spoken to first. He must be an expert on the local countryside as well.

We marched off, Boyle and I, he carrying the map, and I the Binbrook Card. SLOP had gone to Ish and SOAP must have been ishing too, for he was not in his office. At the medical inspection room a man in a white coat looked at our tonsils and painted our toes purple. 'Pinkee Panee,' he said. 'Cures everything. Don't come back.'

'Me track,' said Boyle and led me to the Garrison Church though it was not next on the list.

We found an airman watering a six-foot-high cactus. 'The Nonconformists have one too,' he said, 'but ours is bigger. Padre Epsom is in conference. Try the other side.'

The cactus there was quite as big and the office door was locked. *Padre Derbywinner in conference*, a notice said.

'Me track,' persisted Boyle and it led us to St Patrick's, where the chaplain was supervising repairs.

We've closed a little to a certain extent,' he said, 'but it's only the club that was broken up and I've still a bottle in the vestry. Seven St Andrew's churches, did you say? Come in, come in. Here's Jock himself, who'll know all about it.'

Jock was a lieutenant of the Highland Heavy Infantry, detached from his regiment to defend Tahag. I spread out the map and showed him the seven churches. How could I get to them?

'Me track,' said Boyle, and we all looked round because he'd almost shouted. Or mooed, it might be said, for he sounded like a bullock. He began to read from sheets of paper, and sometimes he mooed and

42

sometimes he whined in a north-country accent. It was about 'a yoong mun and his aaged faather who were sailing in the South Seas.' Their ship was becalmed because there was no wind. 'Ah, where would we be in life without wind?' mooed Boyle.

The young man went for a swim. The aged father, ever watchful, observed a shark pursuing the young man. 'Oh the perils that lurk in the waters of life!'

The aged father cried in warning but the young man did not heed. He cried again and this time the young man listened and observed the shark. He swam faster. But however fast the young man swam, the shark swam faster still. Slowly it was catching up on him. What could the aged father do?

On the ship there was a small bruss goon. The aged father filled it with goon-powder, right to the brim. The shark was very near the young man, with jaws slavering to devour him. The aged father lit the small bruss goon. Would his aim be true? The goon exploded in a cloud of smoke. When it blew away, the shark lay dead upon the water. The young man was saved!

'A fine story and well told,' said Father O'Hooligan. 'It reminds me of a time when an idea of my own misfired. I had my Monsignor visiting the garrison – and he looks a bit like a shark, if the truth be told. We had all the Catholics paraded and we had a fine full church. But the lads were restless, all that polishing of kit and their weekend spoiled. They coughed and shuffled and cleared their throats and made such a devil of a noise that the Monsignor could hardly hear himself speak. There was one of them particularly noisy with coughing so I crept down from the back where I was sitting and I passed a box of throat pastilles along to him. 'For a cough,' I whispered, 'for a cough.'

'And the lad just turned and whispered back at me, "Fuck off yourself!"'

All very well LAC Boyle and Father O'Hooligan converting one another, but what I wanted to know about was these seven churches. How could I get to them? And why should there be seven?

'As to that, as to why there should be seven, it's easily explained,' said the HHI man. 'It's all quite logical.'

'I would like to hear this logic,' said Father O'Hooligan. He brought out his bottle. 'It's your turn to tell a story anyway.'

'It is that we Scots are a fighting people,' said the HHI man as Father O'Hooligan poured whisky.

'I do not see the logic. The Irish are a fighting people too but we've never needed more than one St Patrick's for it.'

'Aye, the Irish will drink a glass or two and sing lamentable songs in their fine tenor voices and fight amongst themselves, which is why they've broken up your church club. The English take their beer quietly and no harm done. But' – he swirled the whisky in his glass – 'let a Scotsman have a single glass of this and he is ready to fight anyone. Whenever a Scottish battalion arrives in a new garrison, the first thing they do is to find the nearest town and beat up the natives. The town can be put out of bounds for so long, but something has to be found to occupy all this energy and the best way is to set them to build a church. It is a task which Jocks perform with enthusiasm and skill for we are a technically accomplished people as well as deeply religious. At such a time there are no denominational distinctions. All are Pregetarians.

'Tahag would have more churches than most places because Scottish battalions are sent as far away as

44

possible from towns anyway. Not that that does any good. They'll still find someone to beat up. So it has to be the churches.'

We sat in silence for a while, impressed by the lucidity of this explanation, But my problem still remained – how to get to these seven churches.

They thought about it and it was Father O'Hooligan who came up with the answer. 'Cultural visits. I've done a lot with that. Make up a party and they'll give you transport.'

'True,' nodded the HHI man. 'Ruins in the desert, rose-red cities half as old as time.'

And that is how it was done. The Brigadier himself expressed approval. Transport was laid on. The Catering Officer promised something special in the way of sandwiches. There was no lack of applicants.

It was the third ruin. We lumbered out in the usual three-tonner, lurching along forgotten roads, stopping to get out and push when the lorry got bogged in sand. In the back the excursionists sat dreaming that they were General Rommel or Japanese rapists. I sat in front with the driver, at my feet a canvas bag with all that I might need.

By the time we reached the ruin it was hot. We carried benches into the shady interior and got the tea urn going. I gave my practised ruin talk and then, after sandwiches and photographs, everyone settled down for a snooze.

I was looking round for some possible place for buried treasure when I became aware of a presence, and there, standing in the doorway, was an Egyptian; an old man, dignified in his galibiyah. Someone was snoring. 'Wheesht, you bugger,' the Egyptian said. A few of the figures stirred but all were sound asleep. 'Minds me o' Pawdry McLeod's sairmons,' he added.

It was one of the great encounters of exploration. 'Ali Mooman Effendi, I presume,' I said. I took the tie and Trophy from my bag.

'Well I'll be dommed,' he said. I put the tie about his neck and the Trophy in his hands. For a moment he stood there, a look of wonder on his face, and then, motioning me to follow, he led the way between recumbent bodies to the place where the pulpit might have been and scraped at the wall with a knife. Plaster crumbled to the floor, revealing bricks behind. A breeze block had been replaced by bricks, and there were wires to pull them out. And in a cavity there was a wooden box. He took it out and, with a certain solemnity, handed it to me.

In the box I found a key and a paper with measurements. We replaced the bricks and scuffed the plaster about the floor and then went outside to sit at the side of the church where now, the sun declining, there was shade. There Ali spoke of his former dignity, how he bore the Holy Book before the Imam and snecked him securely in his box for the appointed time, how he passed round a big brass plate to gather piastres for the Imam while a Bimbashi with a skelly eye watched that none put in buttons. He spoke, too, of Lillie Pasha and the great Ulema of Garbage where Lillie had ruled in virtuous honour. Lillie had sworn that one would come bearing a talisman by which Empires had been ruled and Ali would be its custodian and great would be his honour.

I told him that Lillie now rejoiced in Paradise, reclining on the bosoms of sweetly-smelling houris. He had kept faith as Ali had kept faith, and I too was faithful in bringing him the talisman.

But grunts and mutters gave warning that the ruin party was awake and would be joining us outside. On paper endorsed and dignified by the garrison's rubber stamps I wrote commanding that the bearer of the note should be brought into my presence at any time of day or night without let or hindrance. These flowery conversations are contagious.

Ali and I embraced with emotion and he moved off into the sunset, holding high the Trophy, and singing as he went:

> 'The Ball, the Ball, the Ball, the Ball, the
> Ball of Kirriemuir,
> Fower and twunty naked hures cam trippin
> ower the muir, singin'
> Wha'll hae it this time, wha'll hae it noo?
> Them that had it last time canna hae it noo.'

I listened spellbound. The encounter by the pillar box! *Fower and twunty*, the rune again!

But the excursionists were ready to depart. A last sandwich, a few more photographs of me and Jim at the ruin, and they were climbing into the lorry. I told the driver that I'd sit in the back with the rest so that we could discuss what we had seen. I waited half a minute at the side of the lorry, gave it three smart slaps and shouted 'OK to go!' and then slipped inside the church. The engine hiccupped and roared. They were off!

With the paper in my hand I paced out distances. Plaster! There was an area of floor that was plaster, not cement. It broke up with blows from hammer and chisel. Bricks again, and wires to pull them out. Underneath, an iron plate with welded handholds and underneath that a leather case.

Nothing perishes in the desert. Hence the mummies

47

and the Dead Sea Scrolls and the packets of V Cigarettes thrown away in disgust by the 8th Army and still as good or as bad as ever. The case was perfectly preserved. The key turned in the lock.

Bars of yellow metal. It must be gold! Jewelled ornaments that might have been taken from a church – though not a Pregetarian one. Stones, some embedded in metal, a folder of the finest calfskin which contained documents. I packed it all back into the case and prepared for the journey back to Tahag.

I put my clothes with the tools and the key of the case into the hole and covered it up as best I could. Dressed now in a galibiya, I set off, dragging by a rope the canvas bag with the leather case inside. There was a moon so I could read a compass without matches. The going was slow, up one slope and down another. Sand, loose stones, occasionally bare rock. Once I followed a road for a little way, then went back on to sand and rock following the direction set by my compass. Once I exchanged greetings with another traveller going in the opposite direction. He also had a bag, his carried on his head. It would be a regular route from the camp's perimeter wire. When I reached the Tahag–Ismailia road I stopped and waited. One more hour to the camp gate. It was cold until the sun came up. Then I threw away my boots and the frayed canvas bag and slip-slopped along in Egyptian shoes, carrying the case.

Already there were people waiting at the gate and I joined them at the appointed time for ritual motions toward Mecca. When the gate was opened I shuffled forward with the rest. I showed a note that I had written instructing that 'Ali' should be admitted and sent to the canteen with a suitcase containing church property. The corporal would have opened the case, but without a key and in the face of loud cries against sacrilege, he let me through. I pushed the case through a window I had left open and tumbled in behind it.

In the morning I was filled with excitement as I forced the case lock. The bars, the glowing bars, weighed nine pounds each on the canteen scales. Oh there was money! The stones and jewelled ornaments I set aside. It was the documents that interested me. They crackled to the touch, they must be very old. They were letters mostly, written in Spanish and in French and Latin, some in English, one in Arabic. Quite often the name of Christopher Colombus appeared; Cristobal Colon, the Spanish call him.

But what was this? 'Leonardo da Vinci'. Leonardo? A signature, a letter written by Leonardo! And another that was signed by Colombus! It was an extraordinary collection. Of enormous historical value. Of enormous value in any terms. What was I to do with them? I pondered as I turned them over.

Professor Hubble! It would have to be Professor Hubble. I wrote to him at once. I had come into possession of some fifteenth-century manuscripts, I said, and would value his opinion on how best to dispose of them. Naturally he would share in the rewards. Meanwhile it would be best to keep the matter confidential between ourselves. I picked out what appeared to be a list of Columbus' household expenses and enclosed it with copies of two other documents in a large envelope amongst some tracts that LAC Boyle had left in the canteen. Then I sent it off with the name of Hiddekel Dreerie written on the back.

*

49

A few days later I took the stones to Ismailia where I visited some jeweller's shops, pretending to be interested in buying an expensive watch. I settled on the establishment of Katchabobian, where they dealt with many things in many countries.

Business is not dealt with hastily in Egypt. There are polite enquiries about health. The times are warily discussed, the lack of respect shown by youth to their elders is deplored. Elaborate courtesies are exchanged while coffee is sipped. I spoke in Armenian, and this established from the beginning an atmosphere of confidence.

When I rolled out two stones on to the brass table Mr Katchabobian called for more coffee. I rolled out two more. He poked them gently with his finger. 'Rubies and emeralds.' He took up an eyeglass and peered. 'Not perhaps of the very best quality.' I rolled out another dozen, some with the remnant of their metal setting. He took up one and rubbed it gently between his fingers. 'A little silver.' He stroked another. 'And gold.'

'I have more gold.'

'Gold is always interesting. How much gold?'

I had it worked out in kilos. He sighed and called for brandy. We sipped brandy, gazing thoughtfully at the stones. He called again. An assistant came with a tray on which there was a watch. Mr Katchabobian took it from the tray and, with a murmur of self-deprecation, fastened it round my wrist. I cannot translate what he said. English lacks the subtleties of courtesy.

In no great hurry we came to an amicable agreement and I went off to open an account at the Ottoman Bank.

*

Soon afterwards I had Professor Hubble's reply.

> I have sent one of your interesting tracts to an American associate who is an enthusiast of such things and hope shortly to have his evaluation. Great indeed are the rewards of scholarship and piety. I agree that we should not immediately seek the admiration of the general public. My appointment as Moderator Designate may have escaped your notice. The present Moderator, not being in the best of health, has accepted my offer to represent him on a tour of our overseas churches. I should be able to work in a visit to our troops in Egypt. Let Hiddekel be our password, with Sodom and Gomorrah.

The Chief Constable had read about the finding of the treasure with interest, enthusiasm even. 'Ha!' he said and 'Ho!' and 'Hoo!' He kept a finger on the place. 'What's a Moderator Designate?'

'A Moderator's a sort of Scotch archbishop, sir; a Moderator Designate would be next man in.'

The Chief Constable grunted and resumed his reading, and went on to the end of the story without further comment, save the occasional grinding of his teeth.

The cook rang from the officers' mess. 'Know anything about Burns Suppers?'

'Not much. Why?'

'The officers want one. They're bored with the usual dining-in nights and they've already had kebabs.'

'I think it's past the season for Burns Suppers. There's a season for them. Like shooting grouse.'

'They can't have grouse. What else do you eat at a Burns Supper?'

'Could you make a haggis?'

'What's that exactly?'

'Sort of sausage. Sheep's guts turned inside out.'

'Doesn't seem right for the officers.'

'No. It's a poor man's dish really, what's left of the sheep after the rich have eaten all the best bits.'

The cook thought a bit. 'They could have roast mutton again. It might seem different after a haggis. And they always have devils on horseback.' The cook came to a decision. 'That should do. There's a Greek butcher in Ish whom I've found helpful. We could have a day out on it and then you could help with the haggis. Are you on?'

It would be a chance to deliver the gold to Mr Kachabobian. We agreed to go next day.

Neither New Testament Greek nor my Arabic was sufficient for the technicalities, but the Greek butcher, though alarmed at first, understood what we wanted when we stabbed at our stomachs and bleated like sheep. Haggises are made in many countries. The Germans have them, the French gave us its name, and the Greeks have something of the sort too. There are poor people in every country and there will always be something to turn inside out and stuff even if it isn't sheep. It's only the Scots who make a song and dance about it.

We arranged to call back later for the stuff. 'What have you got in this?' asked the cook, as he helped to lift my cardboard box. 'Gold?' I'd been careful not to leave it in the truck. He dropped me at Katchabobian's and went off to the garrison, where he had friends.

My business was transacted satisfactorily so that it was in merry mood that I met up with the cook again, and when we had collected our reeking bundle I stood treat expansively at a nearby bar. As we headed back for Tahag I sang what I could remember of the songs of Burns.

The road was lined by Egyptian army lorries. Soldiers were trading for sacks of corn and peanuts which villagers ferried across the Sweetwater. We were waved past. ' "Maxwelton Braes are bonnie," ' I bawled, ' "where early fa's the dew-oo . . ." ' We swerved round another Egyptian army truck. ' "And 'twas there that Annie Laurie gied me her promise true." '

' "Gied me her promise true," ' bawled the cook.

' "Which ne'er forgot shall be," ' I bawled back.

' "And for bonnie A-a-annie Laurie I'd lay me doon and dee." '

And the tears poured our faces. Maybe he had Scottish blood, yon cook, or maybe it was that we were weeping for a poor ramshackle army that was going to perish in the sands of Sinai.

While I waited for further information from Professor Hubble I gave what assistance and advice I could to the cook. In the course of this I was myself enlisted to attend the Burns Supper. We were busy mixing and stuffing when the CO himself came to see how things were going. Or rather we were relaxing with glasses of the Mess brandy while Abdul, the assistant cook, did dreadful things to the sheep's stomach. This CO was the RAF's chief boffin and was held in much affection because he never knew what to do with a parade and told them to turn left when they should have turned right and then, with the bright ones facing one way and the dimwits doing what he said, he would tell them to 'About turn!' and when he saw things were much the same he would sort it out by saying, 'No, no, face me!'

He sat down with a glass of brandy that the cook put in his hand and watched Abdul's activities uneasily. 'I wonder . . .' he muttered, 'I wonder how it'll go. Maybe we should have had an ordinary dinner.' He leaned closer to see what Abdul was doing. 'Would you come, Dreerie? I'd be happier if we had someone who knows how these things should be run. We've the Brigadier coming, you see, and the army can be stuffy about things. And then there's the Foreign Office people – you never know what they're thinking.'

I didn't know what to say. 'I haven't the right clothes, sir.'

'I hadn't thought of that.' Abruptly the CO shot backward in his chair, plunging out his legs so that he upset a pail of offal. 'You could come as one of the Mess staff!'

'But I only know about tea and sandwiches, sir.'

He waved a bit of offal that he'd helpfully picked up. 'You'd just stand at the end of the table and signal if anything went wrong.' He brooded over the refilled pail. 'I mustn't upset the Brigadier. I'd be very grateful if you'd come.'

Still I hesitated. This was no time to get into the public eye. On the other hand, now that I had all that money, I'd need to learn how the best people live, how they use their forks and knives. 'All right, sir. I'll do it.'

'Very good of you.' He looked down vaguely at the glass in his blood-stained hand. 'The corporal will see that you're properly looked after.' He swallowed brandy in one gulp and plunged off, looking much happier.

The cook grinned. 'Watch his face as the dinner goes on. He'll switch off. Always does when he's bored.'

I had been receiving messages from someone in a church hospice in Jerusalem; why they came to me I do not know, probably diverted to save trouble for someone else. 'Surrounded. Alone with pig.' 'Food almost done. Must share with pig.' That sort of thing. The man seemed mostly to be worried about his pig but clearly he was in trouble even if he was over-dramatising it, so I sent a message back suggesting he trade the pig for goodwill. Only to be told 'Neither side will offer swill.'

I couldn't give more attention to his problems for I had problems of my own. What was I to wear at the Burns supper? And then I remembered that third suitcase, the one that wasn't mine that the Egyptians had brought into the bus at Port Said. I'd been far too busy to look through it. What I found was a very smart jacket with nice badges and a pair of blue trousers that I could get on, though they were rather tight. A fine pair of boots, too, of a beautiful soft leather. And there were toilet lotions such as I had never used.

I was much admired by the Mess staff when I turned up on the night. 'Very fine,' the cook said, 'but you'll be more comfortable in a pair of my white trousers.'

'And these crowns on your shoulders,' the sergeant said, 'we'd better have them off.'

'You do pong a bit,' said the cook. 'Smell like the AOC on his annual inspection.'

They gave me a tray of drinks to carry round while everyone was assembling.

The HHI man was there and greeted me in friendly fashion. 'I hear you're the Winco's impresario. He couldn't ask me. Never do to have the army advising the RAF on etiquette. I'm to read the address *To the Haggis* though.'

'I suppose you'd rather be with your own regiment, pipers and kilts and everyone speaking Gaelic?'

'None of them speaks Gaelic, and we wear the trews, not kilts.'

'Highland Heavy Infantry, and none of them speaks Gaelic?'

'Och we're all from Glasgow. So are all the Highland regiments these days.'

'I can't agree with that.' It was a captain with pop eyes who spoke. 'Neil Gooch-Fitcher, a friend of mine, is a Garngad Highlander and he speaks Gaelic. And so do all the men who work on his estate. I've been on a shooting party there and everyone spoke Gaelic, sometimes anyway. Neil's mother used to say good morning in Gaelic. *Hammy flook.* A beautiful language.'

'It is a matter of tradition,' went on the pop-eyed captain, 'and that is the army's strength. Every regiment has its own tradition.' He instanced one that wore its caps backside foremost. Another drank the King's health standing on one leg. The Gormshire Yeomanry took all its meals backwards on the anniversary of Ghooly. They started off with port and brandy and finished up with porridge. 'Why, even the Artillery has a tradition. They parade an axe that they captured in Martinique.'

'Aye,' said the HHI man, 'it's an execution axe, and all that they could find when they panted up the hill after our lads had looted the place.'

'Tradition –' But the pop-eyed captain was interrupted by the sergeant's call for dinner. They all bustled about, finding seats, while I took my place where the sergeant said I should stand. The CO muttered something with his eyes shut, and after they had bobbed up and down uncertainly, everyone sat down except the staff and the HHI man who stood watching the door to the kitchen. It opened, and the HHI man began to read from a book. The door hastily shut again as something metallic dinnled on the floor. The HHI man stopped reading. There were scraping sounds and then, at last, they came, the cook and Abdul, bearing between them a great dish on which the haggis plopped and slithered. Three times they marched round the table while the HHI man said something about their honest, sonsie faces. They retreated to the kitchen and the HHI man stopped his reading.

It was a splendid sight, white cloths and candles and glittering badges and red wine glowing. I caught the CO's eye as the haggis was being served out and nodded encouragingly. All eyes were on him to see what he would do next. But the sergeant was at his elbow with a silver tray. Hastily the CO exchanged his tray for a plate of haggis. He opened an envelope and frowned. He showed a piece of paper to the Foreign Office man beside him, and he too frowned. The sergeant retrieved his silver tray and everybody frowned as he marched down the table, tray in one hand, CO's haggis plate in the other. I noticed it is proper to disapprove of what the best people disapprove.

The sergeant came to me. 'CO's compliments,' he murmured. 'It's for you.'

MODERATOR DESIGN BY CANOE TO JERUSA-LEM is what the flimsy said.

Mostly uneaten, the haggis was removed and plates of mutton served. But here again came the sergeant with his silver tray and all eyes followed as he marched again to me. This one was from Jerusalem: SWINE HAVE KILLED PIG.

Above a murmur of speculation rose a querulous voice. 'Yorkshire pudding with mutton? Isn't that rather unusual?' It was the pop-eyed captain.

The sergeant was beside him directly. 'Sir,' he said with cold respect, 'that is a tradition of the Royal Air Force.'

The Brigadier glared down the table. All eyes switched to glare at the unhappy captain as he swallowed Yorkshire pudding with furtive glances at his neighbours.

The younger officers at my end of the table began to talk of wines. They went round France from Bordeaux to the Rhone and on to Burgundy, thence to the Rhine, to Holland and its liqueurs. The loudest proclaimed that egg nog was an aphrodisiac. At that moment the sergeant was nudging the CO who had switched off. The CO switched on in time to contribute something to the conversation. 'Egg nog? My wife makes it for us every night before we go to bed.'

There was a thoughtful silence as he flapped open another envelope and frowned. The Foreign Office man frowned too and everyone frowned as again the silver tray was brought to me. AMENDED MODERATOR DESIGN KANO SODOM. What was the silly old man up to?

The truth of the matter was that the authorities in Malta had been uncertain how a Moderator Designate should be entertained. Would he like to inspect a warship or visit the ruins at Cyrene? The poor old man had a bad attack of diarrhoea. 'Ah canna,' he groaned and dashed desperately for the lavatory. Not easily understanding what he said, they air-freighted him to Kano in West Africa.

The Burns Supper was drawing to its close. The cook

58

brought in his devils on horseback and then a sort of bottle was passed around. But once again the silver tray appeared. This time there was no envelope. It was the note that I had given to Ali Mooman. 'Top secret,' it was stamped. 'For your eyes only.'

Amid a confusion of cries from the kitchen an Egyptian wearing an old Garbagean tie made a brief appearance. He waved the Best Boy Trophy as if to exorcise some evil rite. Pushed by the sergeant and pulled by some unseen hands within, he disappeared. Everybody stood up and sat down and waved their glasses and shouted 'God bless him' and then scrambled for the door. In front strode the Foreign Office man, a set expression on his face.

When they had all gone I collected Ali from the kitchen, where he had been fed on haggis and mutton. I settled him for the night on a camp bed in the canteen. In the morning he had nothing to say about the damage to his church; he had a more pressing concern. The time had come for him to make the pilgrimage to Mecca. With the Trophy's powerful aid and with some help from me, that should now be possible. Could I get him a lift to Suez? I got on to Transport. Easy to Ismailia, they said, Suez a day or two later.

But a world crisis intervened. The Egyptian army trading peanuts with the villagers and that encircled pig in Jerusalem were parts of a wider movement that became the first Arab–Israeli war. There was panic in the Canal Zone, for there was but one single British battalion to stop the expected sweep of Russians and Israelis across Sinai. Those in authority were mesmerised by the illusion that the Canal was vital to British interests. Can one be mesmerised by an illusion? At that time in Egypt anything was possible.

The confusion was compounded by the signals that I had received at the Burns Supper. The Foreign Office man had communicated with London, or Cheltenham I think it was, and lights burned through the night in the offices of obscure departments as their chiefs summoned underlings to execute their ruthless wills. Was the Moderator Design the Russian strategy or a piece of electronic equipment? Scour Sodom and Gomorrah. And what were all these women doing at Tahag? Had the Israelis got their women soldiers that far? And Pigg, who was Pigg?

The HHI man came for me, brisk in action, crisp in word. 'I'll not say *hammy flook*, for if it means anything it means that yon man was wet. As for you, you're in deep waters. The Brigadier wants you. Now.'

The Brigadier glared over a pile of signals. 'Never mind this Hubble!' he barked when I tried to explain the duties of a Moderator Designate. 'What is the design?'

The Foreign Office man was there too with a pile of his own which he tapped with an impatient finger. Sometimes they made a swap, but this was no game of happy families.

I was taken away and locked in a room with an armed guard outside between periods of interrogation. The day was far advanced when they slapped two more signals in front of me, 'MODERATOR DESIGN ISMAILIA TONIGHT' and 'SEND ALL WOMEN THIS HQ'. 'You have one last chance,' they said. 'Tell us who was Pigg.'

They had made it pretty clear that I would not be

back in Tahag, so, when given a few minutes to pack, I stuffed the manuscripts in my case, together with the jewelled ornaments I still had. I think that they had searched my room but I'd kept the valuables in the canteen meat-safe. I addressed my case to Professor Hubble at Flagstaff House, which is where the GOC lived in Ismailia.

I was bundled into the CO's car no less, and found Ali Mooman sitting there complacently. A Military Police corporal got in beside the driver, then we sped off down the road to Ismailia, escorted by a jeep in which there were other armed police. We had not gone far when a despatch rider swerved in front and shouted 'Straight to the airfield! The control tower!'

We rushed on through the gathering darkness, passing through a roadblock where soldiers with blackened faces peered in through the car windows. The gates of the RAF station swung open and we swept on to the control tower. The car door was jerked open, and a major pulled me out and ran me up the stairs. As a door opened to his peremptory rapping, he saluted, began to speak and was waved aside. Someone was talking down an aircraft.

The control tower was in darkness save for one small circle of light in which a hand rested on a telephone receiver, smoke spiralling from a cigarette between the fingers. A voice spoke briefly. Outside, lights sprang up along the runway. The plane came in, touched down and rolled. The voice spoke urgently again. The lights went out and with a roar of engines the plane manoeuvred itself toward the tower and stopped, the engines sighing into silence. The hand on the receiver lifted it. A brief exchange of words followed. Then the hand stubbed out the cigarette.

In a general rush I was pushed out with the rest. The plane, silent now, was surrounded by armed troops. Steps were run up, a spotlight focused.

The door opened. A figure appeared, a small figure wearing a cocked hat. Slowly it came down the steps. At the foot it waited. It was wearing a black velvet cloak and breeches and buckled shoes. From the crowd a tall officer stepped forward, hesitated briefly, then saluted. In the silence his voice was clearly heard. 'I am DOOP.'

'Ye don't say?' said Professor Hubble. 'Take me to your Chief.'

When all the dignitaries had roared off amidst shouted commands and slaps of palms on rifle butts, nobody knew what to do with me. So they put me in a guard-room and interrogated me all night.

A Group Captain, the RAF's senior intelligence officer, offered to communicate with my next of kin. A chaplain with purple patches said he was very busy with conferences. He'd just been at one at a place called Tahag and it had been very wearing, three hours discussing whether their visiting cards should give their hours of services, and they had been interrupted repeatedly by impertinent enquiries about women.

'Well, what can I do for you?' he asked. 'I'm very busy – we have another conference tomorrow. Shall we have a prayer?'

'I'll need to have a pee first,' I said.

A Colonel of the Catering Corps had a good meal brought in. He was keeping out of the way in case they put him in a pill-box with scorpions creeping up his trouser legs, the Colonel said. The Groupie was quite a decent fellow really, he added, but wasn't very bright. The RAF had to find jobs for all these flying fellows when they were past it, and flying wasn't much use as a preparation for administrative work. 'As well appoint racing motorists or bus drivers to high office in the civil service. If they did, the bus driver would be the safer choice. Different for us in the army,' he said. 'We've been looking after our men from the very first. Some have a narrow view of life, straight from their house at public school to their regiment in the army, but it keeps them as amiable schoolboys all their lives.'

There was nothing amiable about the captain of the Special Investigation Branch when he and a large sergeant stamped in. He whacked the table with a leather stick whilst the sergeant stamped in and out, saluting and shouting 'Sah!'

'Pigg, Pigg, Pigg!' rapped the captain. 'Who was Pigg?' He leaned over the table and glared with blood-shot eyes into my face. 'The Stern Gang, eh? Or Irgun was he?'

There were clanking noises in the corridor. The sergeant stamped out. 'Sah!'

'Pigg, Pigg, Pigg!' the captain shouted.

The sergeant stamped back, saluting. 'Sah! There is three wogs as has this note.'

The captain read it and came to attention. 'This note is from the Brigadier! You will admit one of these wogs to the presence of the prisoner. Furthermore, sarnt, the prisoner is not a prisoner and the wogs are not wogs. They are Egyptian gentlemen.'

'Sah!' They both stamped out saluting one another, right hands quivering six inches above their caps.

The Egyptian gentleman who was admitted was Ali, come to say goodbye. The others were the driver of a lorry and his mate who were taking Ali to Suez. Professor Hubble had arranged it. I don't think the Brigadier had been much concerned. Probably he was busy helping the GOC to spread their thin red line along the canal bank to meet the Russian menace.

I was released and taken to Flagstaff House, where the Professor and I were lodged in comfort, though it was noisy with people running in and out. The Professor went through the manuscripts, pawing and rustling with greedy hands. When he was finished he leaned back and whistled. 'For a fac',' he said, 'they are the real thing.'

That night we dined in the Officers' Club, looking over the Sinai, where Russian and Israeli tanks might be churning about in the desert. It was very peaceful. 'Plans,' Professor Hubble said at last. 'Tomorrow we fly to Cyprus on RAF transport. From Akrotiri airport we shall slip away by taxi. Boat from Limassol to Trieste – a Greek ship will be nasty but necessary. We shall avoid Turkey – the Turks are sensitive about antiques unless heavily bribed. From Trieste we shall make our way as best we can to Vienna, where we are to meet my American associate. From previous experience, I am confident we shall not be missed.'

He had moved fast and decisively. And his English had much improved from converse with the natives on that trip to Kano.

Part 3

Alarms and Excursions

'Preposterous!' The Chief Constable flung down the final sheet. 'It makes no sense at all.'

'Maybe. But it's the only clue we've got.' Grue flicked a finger at the pile of paper. 'For this a man was murdered.'

'But it can only be fantasy, all this about a treasure.'

Grue pushed the pile aside. 'Let's go over what we do know. The Consul in Tangier gets in touch with us when Brown is drowned there, for they found the Westerby address in his passport. Nothing much known about him in Westerby. He made no close friends. Always seemed to have money, but there's no bank account in his name. We ask the army if they have a service record for him. They have, and we find that he is the same Brown as the man the police are looking for.

'At the end of the war he was in Indonesia. When his battalion was shipped home they dropped him off at Suez. He served a year in Egypt. At Tahag. And he chose to be demobilised in Egypt. We know nothing of him after that until he turns up in Westerby.

'Potter buys his house and finds this story. Now Boyle appears, looking for the story, it would seem, and he is murdered. There are three things that puzzle me about the story. Did Brown write it? It doesn't sound like what we know of Brown. Then what's its purpose? Why was it written? And finally, I wonder how Boyle knew of it. Whatever the answers to these questions, I see only one thing in it that could be a motive for burglary and murder, and that is the treasure.'

'I say!' the Chief Constable's eyes lit up. 'You don't really think there was a treasure? Gold and precious stones? Priceless manuscripts? It would be something if we could lay our hands on that.'

'It would, it would indeed.' Promotion out of this backwater, Grue thought, taking out his notebook and making a mark. It was an arrow pointing upwards. 'Right then, what have we? We have some names. There's Boyle and there's Captain Gaiters-Gooch, whom you knew. And there's another Garngad Highlander, Gooch-Fitcher. Gaiters-Gooch, Gooch-Fitcher – could there be a connection?'

'There might be. I didn't know Gooch-Fitcher, but there could be a connection. Son has followed father into the regiment. There have been Rhonepipe-Doodles and Doodle-Draynes in it for generations.'

'Sort of family business is it, sir? Like Boggins and Sons, Licensed Grocers?'

Fortunately Colonel Rhonepipe-Doodle was brooding on the history of the regiment. 'I could write to the depot, I suppose.'

'Will you do that, sir? Anything that helps us to understand what truth there is in the story could be helpful. I'll write myself to the RAF and see if they have Boyle's service record.'

Both had replies to their enquiries shortly. Angus Gaiters-Gooch was in California, where he had made a successful career in films, appearing regularly as a bandit chief or the butler in a haunted house. Neil Gooch-Fitcher had emigrated to Australia and been devoured by savage sheep.

Boyle had served in Tahag, the RAF said. They had tried

66

to recall him as an electronics expert at the time of the later Suez crisis but had had no reply from his address of record, the Jolly Roger Tabernacle and Emporium, Bootle. Of Tahag they would say nothing, but referred Grue to the Foreign Office. 'No use going there,' commented Grue. 'The place seems to have been doing something like these chaps at Cheltenham. And you know how cagey they are.'

'Not much further forward then. What's your next move?'

'I have been wondering, sir, if we shouldn't take Mr Potter into our confidence.'

'Potter? What could Potter know?'

'I don't suppose he knows anything that we don't, but he is already involved in the murder. More important, he is an expert in manuscripts – and that is what we need.'

'Well, do as you think fit.'

Grue had not been in the University since the Vice-Chancellor, burbling like one of his own chemical retorts, had summoned the police to rescue a distinguished visitor from man-handling by revolting students. Grue looked at passing figures. Person-handling?

He found the Department of Manuscripts in The Old Malthouse, last in the row of concrete and glass blocks that the university comprised. Potter's office was rather cramped but was given character by illustrated manuscripts on the walls. Behind the desk one showed what appeared to be a game of hockey. The winning team had the advantage of wings and looked smugly down to where the losers registered consternation as a stern, bearded referee pointed to the penalty spot.

'Only a print, of course.' said Potter. 'I wouldn't mind owning the original. Or the original of that one there beside you, the Wilton Diptych.'

'Your work is interesting, Dr Potter?' Grue was careful to give him his proper title.

'Fascinating. But there's no future in it.'

'All in the past?'

'I started with a degree in history and drifted into this.'

'A lot of us drift into our professions in that way. Here's another – Dreerie.' Grue tossed the story on the desk. 'I've brought it back. It's yours anyway.'

Potter turned over a page or two. 'Did you get anything out of it?'

'Not much. A name or two. Won't you go on to a chair from this?'

'A better seat in life? There aren't many in manuscript work and the academic rat-race is pretty savage.'

'Muddy ground is it?' Grue glanced again at the hockey match. 'I suppose it's the same in every profession.' They both looked at the Wilton Diptych. Behind a row of cheerful ladies what might have been vultures' wings were quivering, suggestive of something unseen being horridly torn apart in nature's ruthless struggle for existence.

'Yes,' said Potter, 'I suppose it is. And my work is not unlike your own, Inspector, when you think about it.'

'How so?'

'It's a matter of gathering evidence. In my case it is to follow a trail of errors back to the original.'

'Did they make errors? It looks such careful work.'

'Oh, they made errors. You must see the scribe as he sat hour after hour on a high uncomfortable stool, working by candlelight in a cold stone cell. Tired eyes can err. He might be listening for the dinner bell. He might have needed to relieve himself but have forgotten about it while he finished a word or a line. His hands would get temporary cramp and permanent arthritis. He could have toothache or piles.

'Most of the errors were due to things like that but

68

occasionally someone would make a deliberate change in the script. A scribe might write "goat" instead of "coat" because he liked drawing goats and wanted to put one in the margin. To err is human, but so is mischief. For me, the most interesting thing is to discover *why* a scribe wrote what he did.'

'I have the same problem with the Dreerie story, Dr Potter. Why was it ever written and why was Boyle so keen to get hold of it? I have a favour to ask of you. I want you to read it through again and see if you can suggest some answer. In exchange I've a story of my own to tell and it's a true one.

'It starts in what we now call Indonesia. Before the war it was a Dutch colony but the Japanese took it from them. When the war ended, the Dutch wanted to go back but a strong movement for self-government had developed among the Indonesians and the Japanese had fostered it to cause as much trouble for the victors as they could. A very nasty situation developed, atrocities on both sides. We put in a brigade to try and hold the ring but it was an impossible task; one single brigade to cover all that territory. And besides, our troops were very near to mutiny. They'd already had years of fighting against the Japanese and now they were being flung into a quarrel that they saw as none of their concern.

'In such a situation there were bound to be irregularities, every man out for himself. They say one senior officer flew out a string of race horses as his personal loot. What concerns us now is that a group of British soldiers came across an unguarded bank, or, likely enough, they just shot the guards. At any rate, they looted it of whatever they could take including some gold ingots. All this came to light recently when someone tried to sell a gold ingot in Liverpool. He still had this gold ingot because he'd been serving a long jail sentence for another crime, and he was arrested

69

because currency regulations did not permit the buying or selling of gold. Hoping to get a reduction on his next jail sentence, he named his accomplices in the looting of the bank. One of them was a Private Brown.

'About this time our Consul in Tangier wrote to us about a man called Brown who had been drowned there. His passport gave an address in Westerby. Your house, Dr Potter. We asked the army if they had a service record for him because we wanted to know who would be the next of kin. They had. And the Brown who owned your house was the same Brown who stole the ingots.

'We kept an eye on the house in case some accomplice might turn up. Someone did turn up. Boyle. And he turned up dead.'

Potter turned over some sheets of the story. 'But it wasn't gold that Boyle was after? It was this?'

'That seems probable. But let me finish my story. Brown had a peculiar army record. In Indonesia he had been the batman – that's the personal servant – of an army chaplain. When their battalion was moved back to England, Brown and this chaplain were both dropped off at Suez. They were in Egypt for a year. Then Brown was demobilised and chose to be demobilised in Egypt.

'I've got a service record for Boyle too. He served in the RAF in Egypt. And the interesting thing is that both Brown and Boyle served at a garrison called Tahag. And so did Brown's chaplain.'

'Then there may be some truth in the Dreerie story? Have you been in touch with that chaplain?'

'Unfortunately he can't tell us anything. He died there in Egypt. I have wondered if the truth of the matter is that Brown and the chaplain were shipping home a lot of loot in ecclesiastical baggage. That's possible, the army wouldn't enquire into it and the customs people probably wouldn't have gone through a box of church property.'

'How did the chaplain die?'

'He was drowned.'

'In the desert!'

'No, it was at Alexandria. He was bathing, it is supposed, and was washed out to sea. His body was not recovered.'

'And Brown was drowned too?'

'So it was assumed. His body was never found – just his clothes lying on the beach.'

Potter was silent, thinking it over. 'Then the treasure of Tahag may have been the Indonesian ingots?'

'And whatever else that pair brought out with them from their service in the Far East. But I still don't see why the story should have been written.'

Potter got up and stood looking at the hockey match. For some time he did not speak. Then, 'I'll give you a ring,' he said. 'I'll read the story and I'll give you a ring if I find anything. But now you must excuse me. There are things I have to do.'

Grue left him there, silent spectator of a celestial hockey match.

When Potter's call came it was at an awkward moment. Grue had promised to take his wife to the cinema and was clearing up outstanding business so that nothing could interfere.

'I have something for you, Inspector. Come to my house at six.'

'Not tonight, Dr Potter. Let's see . . .'

'Tonight! It must be tonight!'

'Why the hurry? Surely it can wait.'

'No it won't. Something has been nagging at my mind and now I know what it is, but I don't want it on my hands. The murderer might come back.'

Something nagging at his mind? Something would be

nagging at him too if he didn't take his wife to the film she wanted to see. 'But what is it, Dr Potter?'

'Can't tell you on the phone.' There was a pause, as of one looking up and down the street from a telephone box. 'Come tonight!'

Grue looked at the papers on his desk. 'I suppose I could. All right, I'll be there.'

'Six o'clock. I'll have some tea for you.'

When Potter opened the door he showed none of the excitement that had been in his voice on the telephone. He had ham and cheese and bread ready on the table. He brought the teapot. 'You pour, Inspector. You've done it here before.'

Cheeky bugger. 'Well, what is it that you've found?'

'That'll wait. Tea first.'

'I've cancelled other business for this and I haven't a lot of time.'

Potter made no comment and they ate in silence until Grue put his fork down. He turned his wrist to note the time. 'So what have you found?'

Potter poked thoughtfully at the last slice of ham. 'More tea, Inspector? I could make another pot.'

'I'd rather we got on. What have you found?'

Potter lifted the slice of ham with his fork and dangled it in front of Grue's eyes. 'Ham.'

Grue followed the movements of the drooping pink thing with some astonishment as Potter waved it to and fro.

'Ham,' repeated Potter. 'Pork, mutton, beef.'

Grue stared at him.

'All French words, Inspector. Our names for cooked meats are all French.'

Grue looked at his watch.

'But our names for living animals are Anglo-Saxon.' Potter put the ham down on his plate. 'Pig, sheep, cow.'

Grue slammed the table with his fist. 'What have the

names of animals to do with murder? What have you brought me here for?'

Potter looked earnestly across the table. 'Dung.'

'Dung? Dung!'

'Another Anglo-Saxon word, Inspector, and it sums up the whole matter. When the Normans came over from France in 1066 and conquered England, they compelled the defeated Anglo-Saxons to do the dirty work whilst they themselves relaxed in comfort in their castles. The Normans saw the animals as succulent dishes on their tables. The Anglo-Saxons saw them only as dirty beasts with stalls that had to be cleaned out.'

Potter got up from the table and began to pace about, head bowed in thought, hands clasped behind him. He spoke as one who delivers a lecture often given before. 'The enduring factor in religion is the influence of race. However we may deplore the fact, it is race that has formed our modern churches. The suavity of the Normans, the . . . the angularity of the Angles, the passionate insincerity of the Welsh, it is these that have made the Church of England and the Nonconformists what they are. Just as the social cleavage created by the Norman Conquest persists in names of the animals, it persists also in the division of our churches. For, in addition to eating all our beef and pork and mutton, the Normans appointed their younger and illegitimate sons to high office in the Church, and this continued after the Reformation. The hungry Anglo-Saxons rebelled in the only way they could. They became Nonconformists. This is why, today, one finds so many Norman names amongst the Anglican clergy, whilst the names of the Nonconformists tend to such monosyllabic inelegancies as Gloop and Snitch and Plunk.'

Grue was rising from the table. With an authoritative hand Potter waved him back. 'The variants in Yorkshire, where the syllable "er" is added to denote the practice of

73

some savage avocation, are due to the tribalism that endured amongst the Anglo-Saxons in the North. Hence the abrasive names of Grinder, Basher, Raper, which so often appear in Rugby League football teams.'

Grue was looking frantically at his watch. 'I know something about rebellion. If I'm not back in time to take my wife to the cinema, I'll have one on my hands. For the last time, what have you brought me here for?'

'Patience, Inspector, patience. I'm coming to the point. What I have been leading to is the peculiar nature of the Scotch Church. The Scotch, you see, were not subject to the Norman Conquest, so that their divisions are not on these simple racial lines. They are all Presbyterians – I believe there are six Presbyterian Churches in Scotland. They have beadles and session clerks and moderators and other institutions that are not easy to understand. It is clear that the writer of the Dreerie story did understand them, though. I am sure, therefore, that he was not a private soldier in the army. It was not Private Brown who wrote the story.

'There were two drownings. Brown was drowned at Tangier and his chaplain at Alexandria, and in both cases the body was not found. There's too much of a coincidence here. I wonder if it really was the chaplain who drowned at Alexandria. I wonder if it wasn't the chaplain who drowned Brown and took over his identity and his share of the loot. So the Brown who lived at Westerby was that chaplain. You might well go to Egypt and to Tangier and investigate these things. And if what I have discovered here is as important as I think it is, you should certainly go up to Scotland and have a look behind the fireplace in that college. It seems a likely hiding place.

'One thing more.' Potter put his hand on his armchair. 'For what I have found you will get the credit. In return I shall expect to be kept informed on the progress of the

74

case, on whatever else you find, whether in Egypt or in Tangier or Scotland. Now look at this.' Potter pushed aside the armchair.

There was a hole in the floor. Two of the red tiles had been taken up and there was a heap of rubble. Beside it was an iron box. 'Plaster, not cement,' said Potter. 'Do you remember? He had the same idea here.'

Grue took from the box a weighty object wrapped in sacking and a plastic envelope, a catapult and a tin that rattled. Impatiently he unwound the sacking. 'Gold, Potter! It's one of the Indonesian ingots!' He pointed to numerals and letters.

Potter was examining the catapult. 'Rubber's perished.'

Reluctantly Grue put down the ingot and took the catapult from Potter. 'Vicious weapon.'

Potter opened the tin. 'Pebbles for the catapult.'

Grue ran a finger along the bar of gold. 'I suppose so. What's in the envelope?' He pulled out sheets of paper. '"Leonardo Lesson 1".' He scanned it briefly. 'Something about art. A lesson in how to draw. And what's this? Some sort of plan . . . I know, I know, it's a plan for a septic tank. There would be one here before the WC was installed.'

Suddenly Grue remembered. 'What's the time? Damnation!' He came to a rapid decision. 'I'll take the ingot and leave the rest with you. See what you can make of the papers. I'll just use your kitchen sink. Let me have the page about the college,' he called above the splash of water, 'the bit about the fireplace.'

Potter accompanied Grue to his car and watched him put the ingot carefully beside the driver's seat. Grue got in and started the engine. He looked up at Potter. 'You've done it, Potter! I told the Chief Constable you were a clever . . . I told him you were clever. I told him you'd come up with something!'

Potter leaned in at the car window. 'Who gets the gold?'

75

'I don't know. It'll be a legal tangle. Not you or me though. But you can have the papers. And the catapult,' Grue shouted as he drove off.

Back inside his house, Potter set the catapult upon the mantelpiece. He poked at the stones in the tin. Crystalline. He held one or two up to the light. Semi-transparent. He sat down and turned his attention to the papers. The plan was for a septic tank, Grue thought. Part of it was outlined in red. There was a number on the back. What would that be for? The other sheets of paper were covered with spidery handwriting. Not the hand that wrote the Dreerie story. *Leonardo Lesson 1*. An odd title.

Leonardo Lesson 1

It started with the claim that the writer had invented the cine-camera. He had taken it to Jerusalem, he said, but hadn't used it much there for he was dismayed by other tourists with cameras, pushing in front, and snicking and snocking and dazzling everyone with other apparatus when they should have been considering the meaning of what they saw. And then, on the way home, he was lodged in a long hut at Jaffa and he couldn't pass along the corridor without some other cine-camera enthusiast leaping out like a frenzied tarantula and dragging him into his room to watch films of 'Me and Jim at the Pyramids' and 'Me and Jim in the Holy Land', or just 'Me and Jim'. Finally he threw the thing away because he realised he was only seeing the world through a little square hole.

But it was by looking through another little square hole that he discovered a great truth. It was the entrance to one of the passages that run through certain bricks.

Potter got up to make a cup of coffee. What would anyone look through a hole in a brick for?

76

The writer went on to say that, until he looked through that hole, his portrait painting had lacked the appearance of three dimensions. It all looked flat. But, after looking through the hole, he had painted a wench called Mona Lisa, and he got her bumps right. *Bumps?*

The writer told his pupils to get a brick like that and set it so that it was seen from a little above and to one side.

There is a line running from the bottom corner away into the interior. It is the division between the wall of the hole and its floor, and both are darker in shadow the farther you look inside. If you make a drawing and shade it only to make the shadows look dark, it will never look right. What you must do is to move your pencil in the direction of the surfaces, up or down for the wall, across for the floor. It doesn't matter how light you make it, or how dark. If your pencil moves in the direction of the form, you will show the shape.

And then he wrote about buildings being camouflaged in wartime, covered with wide wavy bands to conceal them from the enemy.

Draw a long flat box that might be a factory or aircraft hangar and camouflage it. Then draw the same box again, but this time shade it. Move your pencil up or down, across and along, always in the direction of the surfaces, and the shape of the box will appear on your paper. The purpose of camouflage is to hide the shape: the purpose of shading is to reveal it.

Could this really be based on something Leonardo wrote? Might there really have been manuscripts such as were described in the story? If these stones were what he thought they were ... And then Potter laughed, recalling Grue rushing off with his ingot. He'd probably left what really mattered. He laughed again, remembering Grue's surreptitious glances at his watch. But Grue was no fool and sometime he would have second thoughts, and he would not again allow himself to be blinded by Potter's science. Just as well if he had his second thoughts in Egypt or Tangier, or at least in Scotland.

But there were things to do. There was a lecturer in the College of Art whom he could consult about the Leonardo Lesson. And then there was that Pring woman whose letter had been attached to the story when he found it. What might she know? He got the letter and a writing pad. He thought a bit. She might need prodding. The Chief Constable's letter – that should do the trick.

He was helping the police in a murder investigation, he wrote. A letter of hers had been found at the scene of the crime and it appeared that she had known the victim, a Mr Brown, and had read a story which he had written. He enclosed two pages of it as a reminder. How much of the story did she know to be true? 'I enclose also a letter from the Chief Constable of Loocestershire, which will demonstrate how much I am in the confidence of the police.'

What the Chief Constable had written was: 'If all would do their duty, as you have done, an outrageous burglary that presently engages our attention would receive prompt and just retribution. Your support has given me much satisfaction. Every cloud has a silver lining.'

'A catapult!' The Chief Constable stroked the glowing surface of the ingot. 'Certainly let him keep the catapult. D'you need a licence for these things? I'll see he gets one anyway. Clever fellow, Potter, always thought so since he sent me that apology. Public-spirited. I'll write to him again.'

'We might find another ingot, sir. I've written to the Scotch universities to see if any of them can identify that college.'

Reluctantly the Chief Constable switched his attention from the ingot to the Inspector's grimacing face. 'Don't look too happy yourself, Grue.'

'A little domestic trouble. We were late for a film my wife wanted to see.'

The Chief Constable grunted. 'Well, keep me informed. Good morning t'you.'

Much public interest had been aroused by the murder. Cars drove slowly past Potter's cottage or stopped opposite while sandwiches were munched. As new rumours spread, interest became closer. Eyes boggled between hands cupped against the window panes. If Potter had chosen to throw his house open to the public for a small entrance fee it would have been a little gold mine. Instead he bought new curtains.

His classes had never been so well attended. Professors' wives invited him to tea. The Vice-Chancellor summoned him to play bridge.

The Art Man was as curious as anyone and readily accepted the invitation Potter had squeezed in between professors' wives' tea parties. He was a rough sort of fellow, not very literate perhaps, but with the reputation of being an up-and-coming man in the world of art. He viewed the hole, then read the Leonardo Lesson. 'Not bad,' he said, 'not bad at all. Stuff there I could use myself.'

'But could it have been Leonardo who wrote it?'

'Could be. He did invent a lot of things, didn't he, Leonardo, things that weren't put into use for centuries. Cars and submarines and typewriters – you'll know more about it than I do.'

'But why would he write a lesson? They didn't write

lessons in these days. Their apprentices learned from doing the rough work.'

'I was brought up pretty rough myself. Did I ever tell you about that?'

'I don't believe you did.'

'Rough, very rough. Kids used to have knives on them when they went into school on the train.' The Art Man rolled up his sleeve to show a scar running down his forearm. 'Knife that was. I kicked him senseless, the one who did it. Schoolmaster too. We was all good friends, you see. But you, are you ready for the return match?'

'Return match?'

'Didn't get what they was after, did they? Could come again.'

'What should I do?'

'Sharpen a knife. Thing is to aim for the stomach, cut upwards, give it a twist. That's if there's only one of them.' He bent to look up the chimney. 'Might be there.' He reached up and tapped the old beam that crossed the ceiling. 'Had any karate training?' He shook his head gloomily. 'Have to be the knife then, and wear steel-tipped boots. Knife one, kick the other.' He fingered his scar reminiscently. 'Made a good team, me and Raper.' He spat into the hole. 'And Boycott.'

'Who was Boycott? The schoolmaster you kicked?'

'No, no, you got it wrong. Raper was the schoolmaster who helped me kick the other fellow, held him down. Boycott was one of me mates. Snooker champion of the West Riding. Seen him knock down three other players with his cue.'

Potter thought it best to change the subject. 'Doing any interesting work just now?'

'Wood. Bloody great beam of wood I get from the scrap merchants . . .' He looked thoughtfully at Potter's ceiling.

'Use the blow torch and a hatchet, splash on paint. Girls too.'

'You don't . . . ? Oh, the girls help you with the hacking and the painting?'

'No, no. Working on girls. They come to watch when I'm hacking and burning. Get a kick out of action, girls do. Show them my scar sometimes. Anyway I've got three bits of wood exhibiting in London, sell 'em for five hundred nicker easy. Girls are hard work. You stick to digging up gold.'

When the Art Man had gone Potter gave thought to his advice. He got a knife from the kitchen and made passes through the air with it. He considered his shoes, which were pointed but not steel-tipped, and painful enough to himself. He dismissed the notion of a man-to man struggle. Yet an Englishman's home is his castle and indignation stirred within him when he thought of intruders and the humiliation he might suffer at their hands. His eyes moved to the mantelpiece. No, the catapult would not do. His weapon must be effective at close range, something that would deter and distract while he summoned help.

What would be the intention of an intruder? Not to search – they had already done that. And murder would be pointless. It would be information that they sought. He recalled scenes from war and gangster films, the victim of interrogation suspended by a rope or tied to a chair, with brutal faces leaning over. He thought of the extraction of fingernails, the attachment of electrodes, and shuddered.

In this low room there was nowhere to hang him from, so he would be seated. They would put him in his armchair for brutal leanings over – an upright chair would be too high. His armchair, so the weapon must dominate an area around it and above it.

Leonardo would have thought of something. Leonardo. A little square hole. He stared at it. Too small to make a trap with pointed stakes like those used by tribesmen to catch wild animals in the jungle. It could conceal something, though, something to surprise or injure. Gunpowder? No, it was too wet, and anyway the intruders would not stand idly by while he lit a fuse. Electricity? He might electrocute himself at the same time as he electrocuted the intruders. But electricity could be used as a trigger to set off an explosion. Whoosh! Potter could see it, the intruders blown off their feet when he pressed a button. What else explodes besides gunpowder? Petrol! Petrol in a can with a sparking plug to set it off. There was a man he knew in the College of Technology who would tell him how to do it. And could the refinement of a scattering of missiles be added? He went directly to seek out his friend.

The Technical Man was quite enthusiastic. He noted heights and distances. He would construct the apparatus himself and would give thought to the possibility of missiles. 'Come back on Wednesday and I'll have it ready.'

With that off his mind, Potter dropped the Leonardo Lesson at the police station. He could find nothing of importance in it, he told Grue.

Grue found nothing in it either, so he took it home as a peace offering to his wife, who was an enthusiastic amateur artist. She gave a little cry of surprise. 'But I've already got this one: mine is printed.'

'Got it? How do you mean?'

'It's the first lesson in the course – "Learn the Leonardo Way". I told you about it.'

'Tell me about it again, dear.' He had no memory of it. She was always talking nonsense about art.

'Two more came and I was improving no end. And then they just stopped coming.'

'But where did they come from, dear?'

'I answered the advertisement and paid for the whole course of thirty lessons. I must still have the advert somewhere.' She shot drawers in and out. 'They were ever so good. You remember I asked you to get a brick? I've lent the lessons to Mrs Puddephat. Look at this drawing.' She showed him a drawing of a face. 'I did that one after the second lesson. That's when you kept complaining you could never get into the bathroom. Maybe the advertisement's upstairs.'

Grue looked at the drawing while she thumped above. It had three noses. Picasso? He remembered bringing her a brick. There had been a dead rat too, and an old boot from the town rubbish heap.

She came down waving a newspaper. 'I've found it!'

Learn the Leonardo Way! the advertisement urged. *You too can be a Great Artist! Send £5 deposit. Courgette Hubble, Bawdy Raw, Foovie, Spuiffshire.*

Hubble?

'Will you get the lessons back from Mrs Puddephat, dear? I'd like to read the others.'

'She'll be at the Art Circle's weekly meeting on Friday. You can come and get them from her yourself. I've asked you often enough to come. It should be an interesting evening. We've got an American artist giving a demonstration.'

When Potter went back to the Technical College the apparatus was ready for him. There was petrol in a sealed can with a sparking plug and battery attached. A wire led to a plastic bulb with a button like a bell push, and on top of the can there was a cardboard canister. The Technical Man pointed to it with enthusiasm. 'Salt.'

'What's it for?'

'Your scattering of missiles. Roughly ground so that it'll penetrate the skin. Should spread around nicely when the petrol explodes.'

'It won't burn down the house?'

'Not at all. Just a little pop. I'll look in on Sunday to see you've got it properly installed. I'm to be in Westerby anyway.'

Potter went off with it all in a cardboard box, and, after collecting his mail at the University, drove home to install his secret weapon. He had two letters. The Chief Constable wrote affably. Miss Pring was less forthcoming:

'It is many years since I knew Mr Brown. I am shocked and distressed to hear that he has been murdered. I do recognise the pages of his story. I regret that I cannot help you. I wonder if you know a Mr Blagger who teaches at your Art College? Some years ago I attended a summer course in wood-hacking under his direction, and, by mischance, cut his arm with a small hatchet. I do hope that the wound has properly healed. His hacking was an inspiration to us all. One felt that Truth was his guiding principle.

Though eager to get on with the installation of his weapon Potter wrote back immediately:

I can understand your reticence, but surely it will be more agreeable to write to me in confidence than to be summoned to the police station. All must be revealed, madam, whether to me or to the Examining Board. I enclose a further communication I have received from the Chief Constable. You will note that I

84

have his entire confidence. As to Mr Blagger's wound, be assured that it is perfectly healed and that he continues to follow the path of Truth.

The Artist blew a blob of ink on to her paper and blew. The blob shivered. She blew again. It wobbled and rolled forward. With relentless puffs she pursued it round the paper. It weaved and dithered, crossing previous trails, and still the Artist blew until, exhausted, it collapsed, no more a blob, just a blot at the end of a wavering trail.

'Such pretty patterns,' someone said.

'Is it symbolic?' hesitantly asked the younger Miss Fitton.

'Ah've trahed Coobism an' Ah've trahed Impreshunism,' wheezed the Artist, 'an' Ah wannid tuh trah sumpin' noo-oo.'

There were murmurs of admiration. Art was so *difficult.*

Grue walked round looking at the paintings exhibited on the walls, wandering lines of ink. It must have taken a lot of puffing. He had the Leonardo Lessons in his pocket. He would read them on the train. Word had come from Scotland that the college had been identified and it was decided that Grue himself should go to look behind the fireplace in its dining room. 'Leave no stone unturned,' the Chief Constable directed. Grue's wife approved the journey too. He could call at Foovie on the way and get her other lessons.

'Last call for dinner!'

Grue settled in the dining car with his wife's next lesson. Appropriate reading for travelling by British Rail, he thought, as he dipped into his Brown Windsor soup and read:

Leonardo Lesson 2.   Discipline to face

I had a teacher once who thought that I was scribbling and, furthermore, that I was uppity and needed cutting down to size. In a museum on a rainy day, while the other students drew what took their fancy, he set me down before a case of beetles. I had been drawing beetles for an hour or two when I became aware of heavy breathing just behind me. A finger stabbed. 'What's that?'

'It's the beetle's leg.'

'It's not a leg. It is a lie!'

Art is truth. Every mark you make should be deliberate and controlled. I have shown that the purpose of shading is to show the form. It is also a means whereby it can be discovered.

If you can tell the truth about your own face you can tell it about anything. So let's begin with that. Close your eyes and lightly run your finger over the surface of your face. Is it not a solid thing? The face of the fair Helen that launched a thousand ships was a pretty solid thing. When that dolt Christopher Columbus had a cold one day he complained, 'I have such a thick head.' So you must draw your face as a solid thing and not as a cardboard cut-out.

Shade gently on your paper, as if your pencil were moving on the surface of your face; gently, as if you were stroking your beloved. All the shading in one mass, no lines separate from the rest, every little bump and hollow. Gently. When it is done you will know the truth.

So draw your face again, but with this difference: draw it from the reflection in a mirror and never once look down at your paper.

Start anywhere and move in any direction, but keep

moving. Wherever your attention moves, let your pencil follow. Up and across and down again, and round each bump and into every hollow, and across again. Keep your pencil moving, but gently, always gently. Stroke the paper as you would stroke your beloved. And don't look at the paper.

When you do look – give it at least an hour – you will see several noses, half a dozen eyes, but one nose will have begun to emerge as the true one, one mouth, real eyes. The truth of your face will be emerging from the paper as you might see a face emerge from mist or smoke.

Grue slept on the second stage of his journey, huddled in a corner of the compartment. Sometimes he awakened when the train girned across a bridge and, wiping condensation from the window, saw a river far below. Sometimes the train stopped and a voice cried from the night, melancholy, incomprehensible, an echo of some long lost battle. Doors banged with the hollow sound of train doors where no train should be.

When finally he awoke the train was grinding across a desolate moor. On each side rock-strewn mountains gloomed. A hairy beast looked up from a peat bog. The engine gave a warning toot. *Choo!*

'Good morning choo,' said Grue.

When Potter opened the door he did not at first recognise the Technical Man, for he was wearing bright green and white clothes fluttering with ribbons and tinkling with little bells. He had a straw hat on his head. 'We're giving a display of morris dancing,' he explained. 'We go round the villages at weekends.'

He fluttered and tinkled over Potter's installation. 'Got it on a good firm base. Wire concealed by mat. Button handy in your chair.' He measured heights and angles with his eye. 'Good, good, the salt should spread around nicely. Now come out and watch the dancing.'

Lecturers at University and Technical College, earnest, bearded, bespectacled, were shaking tambourines and squeezing accordions.

'Stand on your doorstep,' suggested the Technical Man. 'You'll get a good view from there.'

As the dancers lined up, two villagers sidled past. A face peered from the window of the pub. The dancers leaped at one another with jolly cries and clacking sticks and a brave display of ribbons, their bells tinkling merrily. Some children were licking ice cream cones. The smallest began to cry and was led away.

Potter clapped self-consciously when they stopped, but it was only a pause. They were off again. And two were hopping on either side of him. They clasped his arms so that Potter felt obliged to hop too. A particularly vigorous leap carried him backward through the door and, to his astonishment, he found himself sitting in his armchair. The door was shut. A knife touched his cheek. 'A few questions, Dr Potter.'

He looked up. It was a face he knew, one of the hippies from the riot in the pub. Outside they were singing, 'Hey ho, tickety boo, knickers for my lady' or something of the sort, while the knife ran down his cheek and moved from his face, but not far. Potter felt for the plastic bulb. His finger found the button. He slid down in the chair as he pressed it.

A flash, a roaring in his ears. Things flew about. Someone was screaming. Potter crawled towards the door through broken glass. It edged open and bearded faces boggled in.

*

'Morris dancing? Do people still do that?'

'It's a revival, sir. They're trying to reintroduce the custom.'

'So what's the result of it all?'

'The villains escaped in the confusion. Mr Potter had minor injuries.'

'Charges?' The Chief Constable waved his swizzle-stick in a menacing way.

'We can hardly charge Mr Potter, sir,' said the sergeant. 'The villains might have, but they didn't stay to lodge a complaint.'

Someone was watching him. Grue's sixth-sense awareness had saved his life on several occasions. His eyes flicked round the compartment. An old man sat diagonally opposite, one hand grasping a stick, the other raised as though he was about to speak. Grue did not move a finger. The old man leaned forward. 'Are you all right, sir?' he asked solicitously.

Grue removed a finger from his forehead, another from his nose. 'Something in my eye.' The only other occupant of the compartment was studying the rules for stopping the train in an emergency. Grue clasped his hands, twiddling his thumbs, looking out at passing purple hills. After a time he got out the next Leonardo Lesson.

Leonardo Lesson 3.   Of faces and foliage

Things have different sorts of surfaces. You can't draw trees with masses of smooth shading. You have to devise little squiggles for the leaves. But otherwise trees and faces are much the same. They both have hollows and bumps. And they both have facets.

The light falls differently on each facet of a tree, so that it is not all of the same green colour. The important thing is to see where one facet changes to another. There, where the colour changes, a line is drawn.

Where the direction of the shading changes in your drawing of a face, there too a line is drawn. Between the curved crest of the nose and its sides. Between those sides and the curve of the cheek. The forehead has one curve in front and different curves at the sides. The clearest lines of division go from the corners of the nostrils to points just up and out from the corners of the mouth. Very important, these points. From them lines curve up to divide the front of the cheeks from their sides, and two little lines come down and into the corners of the mouth.

Look for all these lines where the direction of your shading changes. Then draw a face without shading but only with these lines. The effect will be of a balloon covered with a net. If you can find the lines and if you can make all of them curve in the right direction, concave or convex, it will be a real face that you see, a face that does not retreat into the paper as an illusion, but comes out of the paper towards you.

This division of surfaces into facets will have been used by Cézanne to paint the Mont Ste. Victoire and houses and trees and apples. And his wife. 'Does an apple move?' he will cry when she fidgets. Geniuses have the same problems as the rest of us.

Potter was able to go back to work, though wearing sticking plaster. There was another letter from Miss Pring. It seemed to have been written in some haste. It began with protestations and disclaimers and concluded with the hope that her declining years might pass without further mention of Mr Brown.

Its substance was that many years ago when she was young and foolish she had stayed at Mr Brown's house, Son Ponce, near the town of San Baccho in Majorca. Knowing that she was a teacher, he had told her of a story he had written on which he would value her advice. It was in a house near Nice, but there was no-one there whom he could entrust to send it. Would she go there on her way home and collect it? He would pay for all her expenses. There were other papers which she would find there too and she should take them all. They were in a cupboard behind a painting of *The Monarch of the Glen*. She must be careful to go only during the hour of siesta so as not to disturb the cleaning woman who was very bad-tempered.

It all sounded quite an adventure and she agreed to what he proposed. She found the house in the village of Loup-sur-Cuddé and the papers were exactly where he said they would be. On the bus back to Nice a clergyman sat beside her, a Mr Boyle, a very understanding man. He invited her to dine with him in Nice and explained what all the papers were about. They had a very pleasant evening, though unfortunately his wallet had been stolen and she had to pay for the dinner. She had never trusted the French.

On her return to England she sent all the papers to Mr Brown. She remembered nothing more about them except that the story smelled of aniseed. She had written a few times but had no reply. Eventually an estate agent called Evans wrote that that he now owned Son Ponce and had she any papers about it or about Mr Brown's affairs? She replied only that she had none.

Recently she had come across the key of that house in France. 'I kept it because I did not trust the post and always hoped to return it to Mr Brown in person. I enclose it herewith.'

In the late afternoon the train stopped at Auchenshuggle Halt. Grue crunched over granite chippings. The man who took his ticket examined it with a suspicious blue eye. 'It will be for to see the capercaillie that you've come?'

'No.' Whatever that was. 'Is there a taxi?'

'If it's no the capercaillie it'll be for the shooting. Whaur's your gun?'

'Not the shooting. A taxi, can I get a taxi?'

'Nae taxis here. You'll have to walk like ither folk.'

'How far is it to Foovie?'

'Nae mair nor a mile, or maybe three. Bonny country, walking,' he called as Grue set off down the road.

An hour's brisk walk past dreary bogs of peat brought him to Foovie, where he was relieved to find a respectable hotel. 'You didn't walk!' exclaimed the proprietor. 'We could have sent the car. Bonny country, though, if you like walking.'

Grue unpacked and went down to the bar for a whisky. The bar was crowded but it was none of his affair if it was open out of proper hours. Attention was concentrated on a man with a long red nose and side-whiskers, who was being urged to have another. 'Come on, capercaillie! Without you we'll be no better than the Laird of Udny's fool!'

'Yon's the capercaillie,' confided the proprietor as he poured Grue's whisky. 'Fourteenth of his line since the battle of Pittodrie. The Capercaillie of Yoker.' He put down the glass in front of Grue. 'There's a z in it.'

Grue looked suspiciously into his glass. 'I take mine neat.' He sipped. Somewhere else the z. 'Yozker? Yokzer? Sounds like one of these foreign drinks.'

'No, no. The z is in Capercaillie.' The proprietor spelled it out – Capercailzie. 'The hereditary name for the Chiefs of Clan Grummle.'

The Chieftain was detaching himself from the others in the bar. 'Just one more, Capercailzie!' someone urged, 'a deoch an doris!'

'I can't.' The voice was plaintive. 'It's nanny's day orff.'

Grue asked for directions to Bawdy Raw. It would soon be dark. 'I'll be back for dinner.'

He came to a bridge and paused to look down at the roaring stream below. 'Sir!' The voice was urgent. A policeman was standing before the bridge. 'Sir, are you going for to cross to the other side?'

Grue took in details. Of middling years, a strong well set up man. 'I'm looking for Bawdy Raw.'

'Just beyond the other side, sir. I'll come with you myself.' And the policeman ran on to the bridge and past him, pausing when he reached the other side. 'The cauld fair gets in you banes, sir, staunin' aboot.' He pointed. 'Bawdy Raw's up yonder.'

Grue joined him. The street he had pointed to was dark, not one lit window in it. 'Hubble, is there someone there called Hubble?'

'Miss Hubble? She's gone, sir. You'll not find her there now.'

On the other side of the road there was a pub, The Claws of the Capercailzie. A few minutes' conversation might be useful. The constable readily accepted the invitation.

The bar was empty except for the man behind it. A paraffin lamp etched shadows between rows of bottles and scars upon the barman's face. 'Ye got ower the burn then, Erchie,' he greeted the constable.

'Aye. This gentleman would like a dram. Glenpuddock, I believe. That'll be twa.'

93

'And one for yourself?' suggested Grue.

'Aye. Fairly.' The barman poured three glasses from a bottle labelled 'Glen Paodaigh'.

'Why is the street called Bawdy Raw?' Grue asked the constable.

'Because there's aye been bawdies there. But ye'll no find Miss Hubble now. She's gone.'

'Aye, gone. But there's still bawdies there.' The barman leaned over the counter towards them and spoke in a hoarse whisper. 'I saw three this verra morning. They was dancin' on the Minister's glebe, dancin' as though it was the spring.'

'Miss Hubble . . .' Grue spoke hesitantly. 'Was she a bawdy?'

'Na, na, no Miss Hubble. Ye wouldna see Miss Hubble dancin' bare naked on the Minister's glebe.'

Grue knew, like any policeman, of the quirks in human behaviour. Curates, vicars, choir boys, it was all accepted now, even lesbian female priests, but this? Dancing? Dancing on his glebe?

'Ah'm no feared though.' The barman's face twisted, accentuating the scars. 'Ah'll be up wi' ma gun the morn's morn.'

'That's it, Alec,' cried the constable. 'Knock her doon, hing her for a day or two, then intil the pot wi' her! And ye could spare yin for the Free Kirk Minister. He hasna a great big glebe like the Auld Kirk mon.' He turned to Grue. 'Did ye want to buy the hoose yoursel'?'

'Is it long since Miss Hubble left?'

'Three, fower weeks. It was jist after the burglary in Foovie Castle. There was a mon cam speirin' for her, a foreigner like yourself, an' she was gone the very next day.'

'Did you see the foreigner again?'

'No. And nobody has cast eyes on him since that day.'

The barman laid a large key on the bar and put down a candle beside it. 'If ye want tae see the hoose ye'll be needin' light. They havena the electric in Bawdy Raw. It's a cauld nicht though for to be visitin' an empty hoose.'

'You'll have Miss Hubble's address?'

'No. Jist a note tae bid me sell the hoose and she'd write sometime.'

The constable was looking through the window. 'Right enough it's a cauld nicht for an empty hoose.'

Grue ordered three more glasses of Glenpuddock. 'There was a burglary in Foovie Castle – that would be where the Capercailzie lives?'

'Aye. It was verra strange. There was nothing taken, but the whole library was torn to bits. They even left the mannyscritts of yon woman's next story, her that writes aboot her brither's schoolfriends as though they was Russian mercenaries or Scottish Nationalists.'

Grue put down his glass. 'I'll go now.' He took up the key and the candle. 'I'll be back.'

'It's the third door.'

The key ground in the old lock. Grue held the candle high and surveyed the room before him. Stone flags had recently been taken up and replaced roughly in an area about six feet by three. The furniture was old and broken. There was an easel made of three broomsticks tied together. A palette caked with paint. Dirty brushes in a jar. Swiftly Grue searched the house. Beside a chest of drawers there were scattered papers and a newspaper cutting with an account of Boyle's murder. Grue tried the back door. It was not locked.

The constable was gone when he returned to The Claws of the Capercailzie. 'Erchie was rinnin',' the barman said. 'They called him on the telephone and he ran. But maybe it was to get ower the water ere the kelpie got him.'

Back at the hotel Grue was greeted by the proprietor. 'Not much of a place, Bawdy Raw, but when they get the electric in it could be something.'

'These bawdies . . .?'

'Och, you'll not get them there just now. Morning's the best time, they're lively in the morning. But you've bawdy soup for your dinner. Make grand soup, bawdies – an onion or two, a leek, a carrot, but it's the blood that matters, makes it thick. You'll not be squeamish about the blood?'

He was interrupted by the phone. 'Aye it is,' he said. 'Is that a fact? You don't say? A terrible thing. No, no.' His eyes wandered round to stare at Grue. 'Yes, he is. Yes. Very well, Archie.' He stood looking at the receiver for a moment, then put it down carefully and went out through the door behind his desk without another word.

Grue waited for a minute or two but the proprietor did not come back. He went into the bar. No-one. He examined stuffed birds and animals. Still no-one came. He shrugged and started towards the stairs. At the door his way was blocked by the constable. Behind the constable the proprietor was gripping a heavy stick. The constable swept a hand across his chest. 'I must ask you what is your business in Foovie, sir.'

'My business? My own. To see a house.'

'Would that house have been Foovie Castle?' The constable held notebook and pencil in his hands.

'It was not. A house in Bawdy Raw, as you very well know yourself. What is all this?'

'Do you object if I look through your room, sir?'

Grue stared at him, speechless.

'Foovie Castle has been burgled and all the silver stolen. I repeat my question, sir. Do you have any objection to me looking through your room?'

Grue's horror at the barbarity of the place boiled over. 'Damn your impudence!' And then he remembered he was on the pitch of another police authority without their knowledge or consent. 'Very well. Look through my room. But here's my identification. You will speak to me as a superior officer even if my business here is not official.'

The constable and the proprietor examined his identification card, looking up from it once or twice at Grue. The constable was neither awed nor perturbed. 'You heard the gentleman, Jimmy, so just you go up and make sure there's nothing missing from his room. You can put away your stick.'

'Oh. Aye.' The proprietor got the message and went up the stairs. The constable remained, rocking backwards and forwards on his feet and looking nowhere. The proprietor was soon back. 'Nothing, Archie. Maybe you made a mistake.'

The constable saluted. 'I'll be about my duties then. Glad to be of service, sir.' He went through to the back of the hotel.

The proprietor was more perturbed. 'That's terrible! I'm from Edinburgh myself, but I like to show true Highland hospitality.' His eyes fell on the menu card. 'At least you'll have some bawdy soup for your dinner. Will you have it now, sir?'

With deliberation Grue reached behind the bar and helped himself from the bottle labelled Glen Paodaigh. 'You'll tell me something first. What is a bawdy?'

'Och, you'll ken them fine, sir, hairy beasties wi' long ears.' The proprietor's English had been slipping. 'Hares is't you would ca' them?'

In the morning Grue walked down to the bridge and up Bawdy Raw. The back door of Miss Hubble's cottage was still unlocked. Another hole had been dug in the floor and filled in again. It was the same width as the first one, but not as long.

A car took him to Auchenshuggle Halt. 'No walkin' the

day?' the stationmaster observed. 'Ye've learned something then that the Laird o' Udny's fool could hae telt ye.'

After two changes of train Grue came to the city. The police there had already looked and there were no ingots behind the fireplace in the college. 'All that way for nothing,' they sympathised. 'That's terrible.'

'How clever of you, dear!'

'What?' Grue was weary and wanted to have his breakfast and a bath. He had just got off the train and the last thing he thought was that he was clever.

'The lesson came this morning.'

'What lesson?'

'Leonardo Lesson Four.' She was waving paper.

Grue snatched it. *On avoiding boredom.* 'Where did it come from? Where's the envelope?'

It was postmarked *Bangor, North Wales.* Grue turned it over. On the back was printed *MacPaodaigh's Fudge.* Mac-Paodaigh? The only thing that had given him any pleasure in Scotland was a whisky called Glen Paodaigh.

Next day he was on a train for Bangor. He had the lesson in his case, slipped in when his wife was not looking. He had thoughtfully put in his passport too. The Chief Constable had grumbled; his silver had not yet been found, and Grue had discovered no gold. And that fellow Potter had blown himself up. 'No, not seriously hurt,' the sergeant said. 'He's gone off on holiday to recover. Majorca, I believe.'

What deep game was Potter playing? He'd sent him on a wild goose chase to Scotland and wanted him to go to Tangier too, and Egypt. Now he himself was in Majorca. What was Potter up to?

Over Brown Windsor soup Grue read the fourth Leonardo Lesson as the train thundered north through belching factory chimneys.

Leonardo Lesson 4. *On avoiding boredom*

Suppose that you were Christopher Columbus writing up your journal of that voyage. Here comes a wave. Here comes another. And another. All the way across the Atlantic. There's a seagull. There's another. More seagulls. That's probably just the way Columbus did write it. He was a tedious fellow.

What would be more sensible would be to note how the waves appeared as the ship moved out to sea and to note when there were no more seagulls. And then say nothing about either until you reached the other side, and again they would have some meaning as you approached another shore.

In the same way when you draw a surface you could put in every wrinkle and every line, and what a bore that would be. Grass or gravel – every blade, every stone? Do rather what the eye does. It switches off when it has seen enough.

Draw again the box that was a factory and shade it to show its shape, but this time do not shade over the whole surface. Shade in a little from the edge to show the direction of the surface, then stop. Stop, but not abruptly. Let the shading fade gradually into white paper. You will find that these areas of white give dynamic to your whole drawing.

So when drawing grass or gravel show the nature of the surface precisely for some little way, then gradually stop. A hint here and there as you move into white paper. A hint again where something catches the eye's attention – a larger stone, a dip in the ground, a plant. But no more until the eye awakens to a different surface or a change of direction.

Roof tiles, stones in a wall, draw precisely at first but then nothing till the eye awakens to a difference. The same with the face. Show the direction of the cheek's curve but let it then be white until you see another, a different curve. Then begin to shade in its direction. The best drawings are those made with the fewest marks.

Grue dozed through most of the long dreary journey and looked out of the window with interest only when the train reached the Welsh shore. Something different. Above barren rocks black birds with red beaks screeched and wheeled. 'They're choughs,' he was told. They reminded him of Potter and his fellow academics. 'Good afternoon, chough,' he greeted them.

Arrived at Bangor he was given directions but found the fudge factory by following his nose. The smell of ripening compost must be fudge. He pushed open a door marked *Office*. Filing cabinets, a roll-top desk, a table on which slept a cat. Graphs and charts and, on one wall, wheels and dials. From an open door came gurgles and spasmodic gulps. Grue rang a bell.

The man who came in answer wore a long grey overall. Not young, sufficiently assured, managerial. 'You're not the usual one,' he said. 'Inspector, is it?'

He knew a policeman when he saw one, thought Grue. 'Mr MacPaodaigh?' he asked, giving it the pronunciation he had learned in Foovie.

'Yes, I'm MacPuddock. What's the trouble this time? Everything's in order. Strictest supervision of the processing. No more trouble with the drains. Have a bar of fudge.'

'Not the drains, Mr MacPuddock, not the processing. A much more serious matter. I have reason to believe that you have been issuing, through Her Majesty's mail, a series of art lessons.'

'The Leonardo Lessons?'

'Precisely so. I want to know how you came by them, Mr MacPuddock.'

MacPuddock scratched his chin. 'It's along story.'

'I've plenty of time.'

MacPuddock looked at Grue with kindly, almost slit eyes above high cheek bones, the kindly eyes of a TV interviewer, confident that he knows more than you do and not caring if you fall under a bus. 'How many of these lessons have read, Inspector?'

'Four.'

'Then I'll bring you the fifth. I'll have to check the vats. You can read the lesson while you're waiting.'

'Just a moment,' said Grue, as MacPuddock turned to go through the door marked *Factory*. 'One of these lessons was found where a murder was committed. Does the name of Roger Boyle mean anything to you, Mr MacPuddock?'

'No, the name is not familiar.'

'And another thing that was found there was a story about a man called Dreerie. Have you ever heard of him or of the treasure of Tahag?'

'Fudge,' MacPuddock said. He put his hand on a wheel. 'Fudge,' he said again. 'The vats will have to wait. I'll have to make a phone call.' His hand slid away from the wheel and took a telephone receiver from its hook. He dialled a number.

The telephone squawked.

'There is no cardboard in the bog roll,' said MacPuddock tonelessly. 'There is no cardboard in the bog roll.' He listened for a moment, then 'Eight-eight-eight' he said. 'Eight-eight-eight.' His kindly smile was fixed on Grue.

'A man called Dreerie?' He put the receiver back on to its hook. 'No, I don't know anything about him.' He turned to the wheels and dials on the wall and tapped a dial. 'Pressure,' he muttered. 'I'll check the vats now.' He looked back at Grue as he went out through the door. 'They're dangerous, you know.'

He returned with a sheet of paper and a bar wrapped in brightly coloured paper. 'Leonardo Five. And have a bar of fudge.'

As Grue sat down to read he was remembering the one occasion when duty had taken him into the grey world where words are passed in the obscurity of code and nothing is what it seems to be. Absently he took a chocolate-coloured bar from its wrapping paper and ate it as he read Leonardo's Lesson 5.

Leonardo Lesson 5. Mud pies in technicolour

Half the fun in painting in oils is its similarity to making mud pies as one did in childhood, the sensuous pleasure of manipulating the gooey stuff. Alas, like other sensuous pleasures, it is expensive. Far better use tempera paints while you are learning. They give similar results and are much cheaper.

My first exercise in colour is to show that there is a relationship between form and colour which is true for everyone and is not just a matter of personal taste.

The three simplest forms are the circle, the square and the equilateral triangle. Draw ten of each, an inch or so across, and then see if you can find which colour best suits each of the three. Start with the primary colours, then the secondaries, and then further modifications if you think they are needed.

You will surely find a colour that seems right for the

circle. You may be in two minds about the square, and you will be less certain about the triangle. This is because the circle is the simplest and the triangle the most complex of the three forms. Try it on your friends. You will not find unanimity but you will find a general consensus. And, given time, everyone will agree.

It is this objectivity that makes abstract art valid. I shall develop this theme in my next exercise.

MacPuddock came back and, after glancing at the dials, sat down at the table. 'Did you like the fudge?'

'Yes,' said Grue, 'but now tell me about the Leonardo Lessons.'

MacPuddock lifted the cat on to his knees and stroked it absently. 'Grandmothers have done a lot for human progress. Watt's grandmother invented the steam engine and showed how to make one by boiling water in her kettle. And Archimedes' grandmother devised the principle that bears his name from her observation of the innocent child gurgling in his bath.' He paused, listening to the gurgles from the factory. 'It was my grandmother who invented the formula for fudge.'

'But where did the Leonardo Lessons come from?'

'Ah, I'm coming to that.' MacPuddock set the cat down on the floor and went to the wall with the dials. 'Pressure,' he muttered and turned a wheel. The needle on a dial flickered up. He sat down again, with the cat back on his knees. 'The formula for fudge is a secret blend of juices extracted from herbs and roots which have been known to my ancestors from the misty beginnings of time. But it contains' – his eyes fell on the cat – 'other ingredients.'

'The Leonardo Lessons, Mr MacPuddock.'

'I'll tell you about them directly.' MacPuddock glanced

up at an old-fashioned clock that wagged upon the wall. 'You must know that I am from an ancient Scottish family which owes fealty to the Laird of Udny. When my grand-mother was bitten by a black adder whilst gathering roots by moonlight and consequently died, my grandfather, no fool as some have said, preserved the formula for fudge. He passed it to his eldest son, who passed it on to his son, my cousin.

'This cousin set up a factory in Edinburgh, and began the manufacture of fudge by mechanical means. Alas, there was a disastrous explosion which destroyed the whole fac-tory and my unfortunate cousin lost his life. He was a man of literary tastes and it may be that such distractions caused him to neglect the precautions which are necessary in dealing with such potent stuff.' MacPuddock rose and turned a handle. The needle flickered further up.

'My cousin was a patriot, a leader in the renaissance of Scottish literature. He lives on in his anthologies of jokes – the point of each explained in brackets. He also composed books of recipes for dulse and other forms of seaweed much beloved by our modern Scottish authors, whose very white teeth chew constantly at dulse on lonely shores.'

'Then it was this cousin who wrote the Leonardo Lessons?'

'No. He was engrossed in astrology. He was forecasting the future when the vats blew up.'

'I thought you said he was writing books on seaweed?'

'Ah, he did that too. A patriot, a leader of our Scottish literary renaissance. On every second page he declared that what he wrote was Scottish.'

'Then will you tell me how you got the Leonardo Lessons?'

'It was his sister's son, my cousin twice removed, who gave them to the general public. On the news of my cousin's tragic end, my cousin twice removed hastened back from

104

Spain, where he had been living, and found the formula for fudge in a bank vault. An outbreak of mad cow disease and salmonella poisoning rendered the times unpropitious in Edinburgh – it was terrible, they said, people were dying like herring in the streets – so my cousin twice removed set up this factory in Bangor. He was contemplating also the manufacture of tinned choughs. And he was working on the Leonardo Lessons which he had acquired in Spain. He had barely completed his historic task when, by a cruel turn of fate, he was drowned in one of his own vats.'

MacPuddock paused, listening to the gurgles golloping beyond the factory door. He looked up at the wagging clock. 'Pressure.' He got up and turned another handle. A needle rose to the horizontal. MacPuddock tapped the dial. 'I'll bring you Leonardo Lesson six.' He hurried through the door, hurried back with the paper and once more hurried through the door.

Leonardo Lesson 6.　*The fat and the thin*

On a good big sheet of paper draw a cluster of rectangles, not too big, but big enough to be painted in. They should look something like the houses in our Italian villages, growing out from one another, not necessarily with straight edges. Do not use a ruler. Never use a ruler. How many rulers are there in the world? And how many of you are there? The marks made by a ruler could be made by a million others. Only you could make the marks you do – and they will be much more interesting even if they're squint.

Colour in the rectangles. Brush strokes, like pencil marks, should always be deliberate and not the camouflage of scribble. So the brush strokes are to go in one direction. This will make your work look as if you know what you are doing and not wandering across the paper like a wet hen. Paint clear and flat without streaks and bobbles. There will be hair marks from the brush, but these will be undisturbing to the eye so long as they go in the same direction.

On a small scrap of paper draw two lines of equal length, one vertical, one horizontal. A difference now? Put in little dots for eyes and strokes for nose and mouth. See it? There will have been two comedians, Laurel and Hardy, who look like that. The fat one is cheerful, the thin one sad.

Vertical shapes are sad, sometimes spiritual, sometimes menacing. Horizontals are cheerful, confident. Any drawing can be made sadder by a slight strengthening of the vertical lines, more cheerful by emphasising the horizontals. Windows with strong horizontals will look out on a cheerful world, those with strong verticals will look sadly out.

Colour should correspond. The colder colours are sad or spiritual, the warmer ones are cheerful and confident.

Draw a line across your paper behind the cluster of rectangles. Colour in the divided background, brush strokes in the same direction, clear flat paint. What emerges is a painting in its own right, for any combination of form and colour becomes art if the intention is purposeful.

'Fudge!' It was MacPuddock with more paper. He seemed unsteady on his feet. 'Here read this one too.' He looked anxiously at the wagging clock and staggered back through the door. Pipes hissed and coiled. On the floor there was a whisky bottle. It was nearly empty.

Leonardo Lesson 7. What to draw.

Sometimes in art galleries you will see the cognoscenti squinting between finger and thumb at some part of a painting. They are looking at a combination of brush strokes which they find as pleasing as the whole solemn painting. Look for the same sort of thing in your own drawings but don't bother about the finger and thumb. In some awful scribble you will discover an area that makes visual sense. It will be because that and that alone is what you should have drawn.

The eye knows what you should draw. The rest of you draws what you think is picturesque. Or maybe it was just that you found a comfortable seat. But probably something attracted your attention.

Draw anything, draw anywhere, and pay no attention to critics unless they are very small children. I was drawing once with a wench and a small child came up behind us. She looked at the wench's drawing and 'That's a good drorring,' she said. She looked then at mine. 'And that's *another* drorring.' Older persons will be less discerning. They will assume that you know what you are about with your pencil and your paper.

When you get home, search your drawing. There will be a part that shows you were interested. Not a whole tree or house or wench, but a combination of lines from all of them. It will cry out to you as the Indians cried out to Columbus, dancing with delight on the American shore, 'Hurrah! Here's Columbus! At last we have been discovered!'

MacPuddock again. This time he had a notebook in his hand and a look of determination on his face. 'I'm going to tell you now how I got the Leonardo Lessons.' He sat down and opened the notebook. 'This is the story told by my cousin-twice-removed. Though it is I who read, try to see a youth unsullied by the wearing world. Hear what he has penned.'

MacPuddock glanced once at the wagging clock and then began to read, the notebook held close against his face. Grue noted that it was a diary published by a firm that manufactured artificial manure.

' "My distinguished relative, the Laird of Udny, desired me to transact business for him at his ancestral seat in the village of Loup-sur-Cuddé in the Alpes Maritimes. Dismayed by the licentious behaviour I encountered in London and in Paris, I proceeded to Nice by the cheapest train. At some time during the night, between waking and sleeping, I was aware of eyes looking down at me as I lay stretched out on the seat of the compartment. I remembered them as eyes like those of a bullock. In the morning, stretching and feeling in my pockets, I found that all my money was gone. Gone too was an English traveller who had eyes such as I have described. Oh, the perils that lurk in railway compartments!

' "After saying my morning prayers I went out into the corridor and looked both ways. The train was slowing down, coming into a station. The corridor was crowded with passengers waiting to get out. And then I saw him, the man with the staring eyes, and he saw me at the same time. The train stopped. He struggled with the door handle and his luggage, dropped everything in a flurry, got the door opened and, grabbing up his cases, descended to the platform. I pushed along to the door but he had disappeared. The whistle blew.

' "There was a moment as the train drew out when I thought I saw him hiding behind a luggage barrow and I shook my fist. This gesture was misinterpreted by a jostled but still courteous Frenchman, who observed that Monsieur's friend had been in great haste and handed me a canvas bag.

'"Back in my compartment I examined the contents of the bag. The Englishman had not lost much. I put dirty socks and underwear out of the corridor window and sat down to read the papers, which were all that remained. There were art lessons, some written and some printed, with a newspaper advertisement which urged readers to write for information about the Leonardo Lessons. The address given was Son Ponce, San Baccho, Majorca, a luxurious Mediterranean villa where supplementary instruction would be given. There were also some religious tracts which, finding them doctrinally unsound, I put out of the window after the socks and the underwear."'

The notebook slipped from MacPuddock's hands and fell to the floor. 'So that's how I got the Leonardo Lessons,' he said from underneath the table as he gathered scattered papers.

'And where were you at this time, Mr MacPuddock?'

'Potatoes,' said MacPuddock from underneath the table. 'I was in charge of the potatoes and had good hopes of being made head pig man to the Laird.' He got himself upright again and shuffled papers. 'What d'you make of this?'

It was a telegram: TENGO DOLORES PUNTO EVANS. Scribbled on it were the words: MOD CONS REDS, HA, HA!

MacPuddock made that hacking noise that Scotsmen make when telling their own jokes. 'It was me that sent the other one. Hack, hack! Did you know that the sanitary arrangements in the Kremlin were installed by Shanks of Barrhead? Did you know that every time Stalin pulled the plug it was Scotland that flushed on his five-year plan? Hack, hack! Shit!' he said, looking up at the wagging clock.

'You'd better read another of the Lessons.' He picked up the notebook. 'Pressure,' he muttered. 'I'll be a minute or two this time.'

Grue waited. Beyond the door vats thrummed and bellowed. A cistern flushed. MacPuddock was more at ease, but still unsteady on his feet when he came back. 'That was a relief.' He dropped paper on the table, staggered to the dials and turned a handle all the way. A needle rose toward a red mark. As MacPuddock went out through the door he was singing: ' "Every road through life is a long, long road . . ." '

Grue scanned the Lesson, 'A journey through colour' it was entitled. 'Fine distinctions of colour . . . opposite to opposite . . . mix, mix, mix . . . turn and come back or go round in ever diminishing circles . . .'

' "Keep right on to the end of the road . . ." ' Mac-Puddock's voice was loud and clear, but then the singing stopped, as if he had forgotten the words. After more noises, the words incoherent but following the tune, more or less, he came back and sprawled down at the table. He opened the notebook. 'Things had turned out so much better than I had feared.' He stared at the page as though listening to voices from long ago. 'Aye maybe.'

'What was the treasure of Tahag, Mr MacPuddock?'

MacPuddock looked under his chair. 'Where's the cat? Puss, puss, puss!' He looked up at the wagging clock. 'Must be in the factory, poor beast.' He stared at Grue. 'A strange story this and it's not yet over.' He turned to look at dials. 'Faugh!' he said, and it sounded as though he was being sick. 'Faugh a Paodaigh! That's our clan motto.' Once again he looked up at the clock. ' "Get out, MacPuddock!" is what it means.' His eyes flickered toward the window.

Grue swung round as the street door opened. A woman slipped in, a young woman holding an automatic pistol. The gun was aimed at Grue.

110

'You took long enough,' MacPuddock said.

'I was in the bath. Who's he?'

'Not one of them. Police. He knows too much.'
She motioned with the gun. 'Against that wall.'

Grue backed. 'Miss Hubble, is it? And Mr Brown, I think.'

MacPuddock was turning handles. 'Pressure.'

'There's gold still in the vats,' the woman said.

'Only one ingot. There's more at stake than that and we're well insured.'

'Through that door,' the woman ordered. 'Are you going to say a prayer?' she asked MacPuddock. 'That would be nice.' Her voice was throaty, French.

The street door slammed open behind her and a gun coughed twice. She was flung forward and fell sprawling. MacPuddock jerked. Slowly, wearily, he leaned over the table and rested his head upon the notebook. 'Faugh,' he sighed, or 'fudge' it might have been.

The man at the door closed it quietly, pistol probing the room. He moved toward the table, considering Grue. Then he brought out a long thin knife and slid the pistol into his belt. Without taking his eyes from Grue he pulled the notebook from under MacPuddock's head.

In the factory metal screeched and wrenched In that moment of distraction Grue went on the attack, his foot hard on the man's instep as his fingers prodded toward the eyes, swivelling as the knife came in and aiming a hard chop at the throat, then once again. The knife dropped, the man was crumpling. Grue struck again and kicked him once on the side of the head. He stooped and lifted the head by the hair. Finished.

Metal screamed again and groaned. Grue searched the bodies and put money on the table, Spanish and French. He dragged the bodies through the factory door. The vats were rumbling. Something hissed and spat as he ran back and snatched up the money and the notebook, and ran out into the street. The factory blew up when he was a hundred yards away.

Grue waited quietly in the station as fire engines clanged through the streets. A pall of smoke lay above the town. There was a nasty smell.

On the train to London Grue studied MacPuddock's notebook. All that was written in it were jokes and recipes. Grue read the first three recipes – stuffed seaweed, dulse poitevine, seaweed kebabs – and went to the buffet for a sandwich. He read three of the jokes.

1. The Minister asked Sandy why he had not been in church last Sunday. 'It was raining,' Sandy said. 'But it was dry inside,' said the Minister. 'Aye, that was another reason.' (It was raining so it was wet outside but it was not raining in the church so it was dry there. And the Minister's sermon was dry too!)
2. The Minister met a farmer and said, 'How wonderful that God feeds even the little sparrows!' 'Aye,' said the farmer, 'off my oats!' (The sparrows eat oats. God makes the oats grow but so does the farmer! There is a very interesting theological point here.)
3. I don't quite understand this one myself. The Egyptians invented the bagpipes for a joke. They gave them to the Irish for a joke. The Irish gave them to the Scots for a joke. But the Scots haven't seen the joke yet.

Grue ran his eye over some others. The point of each was carefully explained in brackets, except for the one about the bagpipes.

Nothing else was written in the notebook, but there were loose sheets of paper, a picture postcard and the business

112

card of an estate agent in Majorca. The postcard showed a walled village on a hill. On the back its name was given as Loup-sur-Cuddé, Alpes Maritimes. There was a brief message, *This is what you must remember.* That spidery writing again. No address or signature, just a telephone number.

Grue disposed of the jokes and recipes in the proper place and dropped the rest of the notebook out of the corridor window. Back in his compartment he read the loose sheets of paper. There was another story, this one in the same spidery writing, and two letters.

The first letter was from an address in Vienna to 'Dear Mr Brown' and was signed 'Gertrud Büstj'.

The Professor returned while you were in custody. He was looking for manuscripts, which Mr Hubble must have taken. Their loss made Mr Hubble quite sad but mostly he was exuberant. He insisted that we go that night to drink the new wine at Grinzing. When I came to the Slurpenstrasse, dressed for the occasion, he was already drunk. He put on strange garments such as are worn at village festivals and performed a peasant dance – 'The Mountain Throw', he called it. Dr Wettstein and I refused to join him in this and, after we had persuaded him to dress more conventionally, we set out. As always, I was moved to be walking on the path where Beethoven composed his great music but all that the Professor wanted was to find some weinhaus where he could hear the music of Johann Strauss. In the early hours of the morning we returned to the Slurpenstrasse and, the others being asleep with wine, I searched the Professor and his luggage. It is clear that he has opened an account in Switzerland. I also found this telegram, which I have not understood. I regret that we had no opportunity to discuss these matters before the police expelled you from Austria. It will be to our common interest to do so. Meantime inform me of the address of Mr Hubble if you have it. I have a strong passion for him. Dr Wettstein has been drowned in the Danube. Strauss, hah!

The second letter was written from the village shown in the picture postcard and was signed 'Gertrud Hubble'.

Dear Brown, I despair of what is to become of me and my dear Courgette. I would push the old fool down the stairs if only I could find where he hides his secrets. I have offered fair exchange, my secrets for his, but he will reveal nothing. Does he not care that we starve? Is it for this that I married the old goat?'

Grue turned to the story. It was a very long one.

I have entrusted this, my dear Courgette, to Maître Heyraud and it will be delivered to you only when I am dead. It concerns the Leonardo Lessons. As you know, they were my financial support in Spain and it was one of my pupils, the Capercailzie of Yoker, who gave us our house here. The Lessons will provide you with a living, though in due course you will find something else. A word of advice. Do not place your advertisements in *Vogue* or *The Times*. Subscribers for correspondence courses are more likely to read *The New Statesman* or the *Observer*.

And do not offer supplementary summer courses. Only two of my pupils took up that offer but it caused a lot of trouble. They were two ladies from Wimbledon and, as you shall hear, they had not come for my courses at all. Since they were English ladies I had to make changes in my way of life. Beds had to be bought, and a teapot, and a bath, which fell off the cart half way up

114

the hill and spun down the track like a demented Swiss until I could catch hold of it. But it was the earthen closet which had no door. And you can't have English ladies squatting in public view. So I set about the construction of a septic tank which would receive necessary drainage from bathroom apparatus. I laboured over that septic tank for weeks until it became apparent that I could not finish it in time. What I recall most vividly was a pipe that leaned against the wall and sneered like a trades unionist who would do no other man's work.

I considered alternatives. Beer bottle caps on strings as screens like those some bars employ, but I just did not drink that much beer. I settled on lengths of steel chain, very pretty, they swayed with a glamorous effect that might bring to the ladies' minds thoughts of Arab sheiks and milk-white camels in the desert. And indeed, when the ladies came, they were quite delighted. It was a change from Wimbledon.

Things had turned out so much better than I had feared. It was a shock then when they interrupted me as I began to explain the first part of their lessons, and said that they had not come to do my course at all, but to visit Henry Tombs, who lived just along the coast. They had written a novel and had sent it to him for his opinion. I told them that Tombs was an old goat with a harem of young girls and he wouldn't give them the time of day, but they were adamant. He was a distinguished man of letters, they said. And they set out, hardly pausing after breakfast, save for the normal hesitations, preparations and reconsiderations of female persons bent on an excursion. They carried bright bags and lotions. They knew not when they might return. They would picnic by the sea.

It was very late when they came back. They were weary and indignant. Mr Tombs was not a nice man and I should have warned them. And he had lost the script of their novel. They would start on my course the next day, they said, and so they did.

In old age I find it difficult not to get confused between the Lessons and the septic tank and the ladies having their picnic in the cove below Henry Tombs' house, among his harem. Let me go on now to tell you how I got the Leonardo Lessons. There is more that you should know and you will be informed when the time is right. And you must get from your mother whatever information she has.

Not long after the war ended I was teaching English at a language school in Trieste. It was run by a man of questionable origins. Some said that he had been a war criminal and I know that he had been in Croatia during the fighting there. He once told me he was a crack shot, but that was when I asked him for a rise in salary and I may have misheard the vowel. His qualifications appeared to be only those certificates that people get when they have failed at school and want to get into an English university. He had them hanging on his office wall.

Trieste attracted odd characters. Burton was our Consul there – the explorer, not the one who shouts so loudly in those films. And there was James Joyce, who was a writer of some sort, and there was an Italian who kept starting wars. I was not too surprised, then, when two odd characters walked in and asked if I could put them up for a night or two. The younger one was called Brown. The old man was known to me only as the Professor or the Maude – never, for some reason, as Professor Maude. They had ready money, so I took them in, a camp bed for the old fellow and Brown slept on the floor.

That night I must have gone on a bit about my job

116

and made it clear that I would be glad to escape from Trieste, for, after we had talked a while, the two of them exchanged a long look and the old man nodded and put it to me. How would I like a trip to Vienna, all expenses paid and a hundred pounds more for my trouble?

They had come off the boat from Cyprus, so it could have been drugs. I hummed and hawed until they held out fifty pounds. I'd get the other fifty in Vienna. They said that their problem was some valuable manuscripts that the Professor wanted to compare with similar ones in Vienna. They would have to pass through the Russian zone of occupation and the Russians were in the way of confiscating from travellers anything that took their fancy. With three of us together, we could switch our cases about at the checkpoint. Much safer with three, they said.

I didn't know what to make of it, but a hundred pounds was a lot of money in those days, so I agreed to go. They got my passport stamped the next day, a whole page with the American eagle all over it. And they got me a thing called a grey card, which was needed to get into Vienna. They must have had some influence.

We left late that night, travelling in the back of a NAAFI truck. Most of the way I slept, but I woke once when a light flashed on my face and voices spoke in German. We stopped for a while in a village for something to eat, then went on through a town called Klagenfurt to a smaller town on the railway line. The train we got on to had only wooden seats and it was crowded, but room was made for us. I was becoming worried about what I'd let myself in for, the more so when I saw the Austrians rearranging their baskets and cases and looking worried too. What would happen at the checkpoint? I asked.

'Nothing to worry about,' said Brown. He took down a case and opened it. 'This is what you will show.' There were a few socks and shirts and underwear, two tins of processed meat and a bottle of whisky. There was also a large envelope, stamped *Canteens for HM Forces*, with words in German and in Russian that must have said the same. 'But be ready for a last minute switch,' Brown said.

'Switch to what?' I asked, not liking this at all.

'Switch to your own case, but only if I give you the nod. Oh, and protest when they take the whisky, but not too much.'

The train began to slow down, went on for a while in spasmodic jerks, and finally ground to a halt in a cutting. Doors banged and there were peremptory shouts, metal rapped on glass along the corridor and then they came to our compartment, large men in heavy coats. One strode in and glared around. From one Austrian he took a cheese, from another a bottle of wine, and passed them out to a colleague, who put them in a sack. He pointed to the case that Brown had opened. No sign from Brown. I got it down. The guard passed the tins of meat and the whisky out. He lifted out the envelope and let it drop back. I muttered protests, but he was pointing to the case that was really mine. Brown got it down. Nothing there of interest. He pointed to the Professor's case.

The Professor was a little man. He could not reach the rack. The Russian grabbed it himself and flung it open on the seat. We all watched with some astonishment as he lifted out old-fashioned clothes, purple and black silk, and a cocked hat and buckled shoes. Another envelope too, the same size as the one that I had shown, but without official stamps. The Russian stood, the envelope in one hand, the cocked hat in the

118

other, and suspicion on his face. He came to a decision, just as a British customs officer would have done. It was unusual, so it had to be wicked. He ripped the envelope open. He pulled out sheets of paper covered with writing in English and little diagrams. He roared. His colleague rushed in from the corridor. They grabbed the Professor by both arms and dragged him away despite all our cries of protest. Brown was quite unperturbed. 'Don't worry. The Maude can look after himself.'

Soon afterwards the train started off again and in a short time was clanging into the station in Vienna. Brown led me through a maze of streets to one that was called Slurpenstrasse and to a doorway propped by wooden beams. Brown knocked in a predetermined way and the door was opened by a grim grey man with only one arm. There were muttered introductions and we were shown into a bedroom. Brown sat down on one of the two beds, counted fifty pounds from his wallet and held them out. I had done my job, he said, and I could go.

Having come that far, though, I wanted to see something of Vienna. I was curious, too, to know what had happened to the Professor. Could I not stay on a day or two? I asked. All one to him, Brown told me, it would depend on our host, Dr Wettstein. He himself would be occupied with his own business.

Rather grudgingly, the man with one arm gave me a key. That evening and next day I explored the city, wandering through the little streets of the old part, mostly, where the ochre-coloured walls were still blackened by the fires of war. I did not seek out the famous buildings, but when I came to the National Library I recalled that it was there that the Professor was going to make comparisons of manuscripts, so I went in with the vague hope of finding him. But it was Brown I saw. He was leaning over a display case, pointing and muttering to a young woman beside him. He did not seem too pleased to see me but introduced his companion as Fräulein Büstj. I withdrew after a few remarks of no consequence and that is all I saw of your mother, my dear Courgette, until she arrived at Loup-sur-Cuddé, determined to be my wife.

As I turned out of the gallery I was swept aside by men in uniform – uniforms, I should say, for, like everything in Vienna at that time, it was a joint movement of Russians, Americans and British. French too, I do believe. Anyway, they rushed together to seize Brown. The Fräulein had disappeared. I made my own departure hurriedly and returned straightway to the apartment in the Slurpenstrasse. My one thought was to collect my case and get out of Vienna, away from whatever it was I was mixed up in.

There was no one in the apartment. I looked around a bit, not spending too much time on it. What I found was an envelope containing very old manuscripts. I thought it might as well be me who took charge of them. These manuscripts related to the work and views of Leonardo, and it was from them that I derived the correspondence course which I have called the Leonardo Lessons. By selling them I raised the money to buy a suitably remote house in Spain and to support myself until the lessons could.

The story ended with expressions of affection.

Judges stare from benches, Headmysteries on schools assembled. Innocence and guilt both crumple. From its high post the staring owl listens for the squeak of self-betrayal, then descends the rending beak. The Byzantine emperor who holds Holy Wisdom in his hand stares stonily, having other things in mind. So Grue stared and paper crumpled in his grasp. Would it again be Brown Windsor soup?

Part 4

An Alliance Reached

On the plane to Nice Grue studied a map that he had bought in London. There was a path that led up from the coast to the village of Loup-sur-Cuddé, starting from quite near the airport. It would probably be quicker than public transport and more discreet, and there was a railway station where he could leave his case.

It was rough going but there was a pleasant scent of herbs and no bogs of peat. Bonny country, if you liked walking. He crossed a single-track railway line, apparently disused, and there above him was the village, just as it was shown on the picture postcard. A last steep climb took him to an arched gateway in the wall. He passed through and, by a narrow street, came to the village square where a large sign confirmed that he was in Loup-sur-Cuddé and informed him further that it was *La Ville des Grummles*. Well, well, well!

In the Bar du Cuddé he was given the explanation. The Grummles were a noble Scottish family who had fought valiantly for France in the wars against the English, and for this the King had given them a château in the neighbourhood. In later wars involving the Dukes of Savoy and the Grimaldis and various holy but avaricious Popes the château had been completely destroyed, but the Grummles retained a house in the village itself and the people of the village cherished the association. Its very name derived from the heroic exploit of a Chieftain of the family who had made a prodigious leap from the wall of the village on to his horse and so escaped his enemies. 'Loup' was the Scottish word for leap, explained the patron, and a Scottish horse is called a 'cuddé.' Grue was urged to see the house of the Grummles and was directed to the Rue du Grand Loup.

The house could not be mistaken. Above the door was sculpted a great bird with a motto clasped in its talons:

> Matthew, Mark, Luke and John
> Haud the cuddy ere I get on.

A capercailzie! Here was the link between Grummles and Hubbles and MacPuddock! What secrets might that silent house reveal? Grue paused only long enough to note that the old door had been fitted with a modern lock.

That night he dined in the Hôtel des Grummles on *civet de lièvre*, cooked according to a recipe handed down from father to son by the chaplains of Clan Grummle. He lingered on over a second bottle of the rich red Château Fouvet before making his way back through the archway in the wall to find a secluded place where he could wait unobserved. When the bells sounded midnight he returned to the house of Clan Grummle. The street was deserted, lit by one wavering lamp, and the house was silent. He had no trouble with the lock.

He found only two things of interest downstairs. There were two gold ingots under the kitchen sink. And in a locked cellar below the stairs there was a variety of weapons and explosives. His foot was on the first step to go upstairs when he heard a snore. Someone was in the house! Grue went on up very quietly. Behind a closed door the sleeper snored on.

From another bedroom there were other stairs winding steeply up to a terrace in the open air. On one side the roof rose steeply. On the other the village wall fell sheer to the ground. Grue brought up the ingots and dropped them over. One lay gleaming on a path, the other clinked against something and rolled out of sight.

He let himself out into the street. A path led round the foot of the wall and not far along it he saw the first ingot and found the other. He carried them to his former hiding place and thrust them deep into the bushes. The village clock struck one as he set off down the path in darkness toward the sea. Eventually he came to the station where he had left his case and dozed there on the platform till the first train came.

Potter had been dreaming he was in prison and when he awoke he was facing a stone wall. He sat up with a start. He found he was in a comfortable bed, far more comfortable than the one in Grue's cell, and remembered where he was. He dressed hurriedly and went downstairs. No tea or coffee in the kitchen. He looked under the sink. No ingots either! And then he heard a key scratching at the front door lock.

The rope! There was a rope in the cupboard half way up the stairs! He was round the turning when he heard the door open. For the moment out of sight he dragged out the rope and hauled it up to the bedroom, where other stairs went up to a platform in the open air. Once up and out, he tied one end hurriedly to an iron bracket in the wall and pushed the rest over. It was a long way down. Before thought could stop him he was over the parapet and sliding down the rope. As it did not reach the ground, he hung there a moment, swinging, then dropped the last few feet. Looking for a way down to the sea, he found a path and followed it downhill. He saw no one but a sleeping figure on a railway platform. Some tramp likely, he thought. Thank goodness selling those stones in London had given him the means to do his travelling by air.

Grue booked in at a hotel in Marseille and then phoned the estate agent, Evans. Yes, said Evans, he did know Brown. And yes, Grue could see Brown's house. Evans would meet him at San Baccho railway station at lunchtime in two days' time.

That evening after dinner Grue walked round the Old Port. He could see the island from which the Count of Monte Cristo had escaped. There's always a way of escape, he mused, and the resolute get out.

A night in Palma de Majorca after the boat trip across and a short railway journey in an old-fashioned train brought him to San Baccho. Looking round as he came out of the station, he easily picked out Evans. There was something familiar about the figure standing at a precise angle of thirty degrees from the main entrance, feet astride, hat clasped over stomach. Yet Grue was sure he had never seen that well-scrubbed face before.

'Good trip?' Evans took the case and opened the car door. He smelled of deodorant. 'We've a lot of expatriates who've settled here, English, Dutch, German, Australians. Retired people mostly, some of them quite distinguished,' he began amiably as they drove out of the town. What sort of property did you have in mind? Brown's place wouldn't suit you – too far into the sticks. But I can find you something better. Did you know Brown well?'

'Hardly knew him at all.'

They came to a village and drove into the square. Evans parked the car in the shade of a high wall and took Grue up a flight of steps into a narrow lane. As they passed a bar from which loud music blared, a young woman came out and Evans greeted her affably. 'That was Brown's woman,' he said. 'They say her child was his.'

Grue glanced back. She was slip-slopping away along the lane, buttocks churning to the music from the bar: ' "These-were-the . . . days-my friend . . . we-thought-they'd-ne . . . ver-end . . ." '

'How does she support herself?'

'Begonia? Oh, the usual way, and Brown probably settled something on her.'

They climbed more steps and passed through wrought-iron gates set in a high wall. A gardener who was dragging a hosepipe between orange trees saluted Evans. Then they sat on a terrace where it was cool after the heat of travel, and a maid brought drinks. Only the hiss of water from the hosepipe and the distant music from the bar disturbed the silence.

'You say you didn't know Brown well?'

'People who lived near him were friends of mine and told me about his house here. Why do you think it wouldn't suit me?'

'No proper door or windows. Earthen floor. No electricity and only a well for water. It's all in poor repair and you can only get to it by walking. What did your friends say about it?'

'They gave me the impression it was fairly grand. But they didn't know Brown all that well either. He kept mostly to himself, they said. What business was he in here?'

'Import-export, you could call it.' Evans stared at Grue. 'What business are you in yourself, Mr Grue?'

'Insurance.' Grue grimaced. 'It's not an exciting way of life but it's a safe one. I'm a careful person.'

Still Evans stared. 'Do you have any papers of Brown's?'

'No. Why? Is there some difficulty about buying the house?'

'None at all. Effectively, I'm the owner.' Evans paused. 'Well, there could be a difficulty. I think I'd better tell you about Brown's import-export business. Fact of the matter is he was a smuggler.'

'What – carrying barrels of brandy into a secret cave?'

'No, it wasn't like that at all. This was big. American cigarettes, guns for the Arabs, drugs maybe, and gold – there's always a market for gold. You could buy these high-powered speedboats cheap just after the war, things that could outrun anything the customs people had.' Evans paused again. 'Brown was in with a queer lot. And then he got in trouble with them. He made off with one of the boats.'

'That would represent a lot of money?'

'It did. It was mostly a cargo of gold.'

'My friends said he drowned at Tangier. That's why they thought I'd get the house cheap. D'you suppose his partners caught up with him there.'

'Nobody knows what happened in Tangier. He came back here before that though, as bold as brass, with some story about the boat being hijacked by someone else. His partners pretended to believe him. They thought that if they had him under their eye they might get the boat and its cargo back. What happened, I think myself, is that he sank it. Brown wasn't very clever, and yet he was clever about some things. There was another fellow who was living with him at Son Ponce and he went soon afterwards to France. Brown thought that this fellow had papers of great value, papers that concerned something they'd been up to in Vienna. So what Brown did was to write a story containing hints that he himself had secret information. He soaked the story in aniseed and sent it to the fellow in France. Then he got a man called Boyle to go to the house in France disguised as a clergyman, taking with him a dog. While this

128

Boyle was prosing on, the dog went sniffing and revealed where there was a secret hiding place in that French house. After that it was just a matter of burglary.'

'I'd no idea that Brown was involved in things like that. It makes me all the keener to see his house. It'll be something to tell my friends about.'

'I suppose so.' Evans leaned across the table and put his hand on Grue's arm. 'If you do have any papers . . .'

'No, I haven't any papers. What sort of papers would they be?'

'I'm not sure. But I do know that Brown's former associates would be very grateful for anything of the sort, very grateful.' Evans looked thoughtfully at Grue. 'I'd be pleased to act as intermediary.' He drew back. 'You should know that these people could be dangerous if anyone got in their way.'

'No, I don't know anything about it. But I'd still like to see Brown's house. It'll be quite a story to tell my friends.'

'I suppose so.' Evans poured the last of the bottle of wine. 'All right, Mr Grue. You'll see Son Ponce.' He lifted his glass in salutation. 'A careful person, are you? That's good. You'd better be careful when you're at Son Ponce. And afterwards . . . I may find you something more suitable. We'll have lunch now. You must be ready for it.'

Over lunch Evans talked of his war-time travels. 'Got out of the Far East before the Japs came. Then went to the Middle East, a bit of Africa. They gave me a priority card in Cairo so I could get on any flight I wanted. Once I was challenged for my seat by a full colonel but Jock Whitney was on the plane and saw him off. Left him fuming on the tarmac. I met Churchill in Tripoli, ran into him again in Marrakesh. "You're always turning up," he said. Smoked these big cigars all the time. I still have the butt of one he gave me. Kept it as a souvenir.'

It was all rather overpowering and Grue was feeling the effects of his journey, and the wine. 'Could you fix me a hotel room?' he asked at last.

'I'll do it right away. You'll go to Son Ponce this afternoon?'

'As soon as I've had a shower.'

'You'll have to walk. I'll draw you a map when I've phoned.'

Evans was away for quite a time, his voice murmuring on a telephone. Grue looked round the photographs in the room. Many were of people who were famous, some were signed. Grue went down the steps and took a turn round the garden. He was bending over a bed of begonias when Evans appeared on the terrace. 'All fixed. Hotel Bristol. They're sending a taxi.'

While they waited Evans drew a map. 'You go out of town by this road, the Pucha road, and there you'll see a ceramics works – you can't mistake it, pots all around. Turn off on the *camino* – that's an unmade road – and follow it for a mile until you come to a big walnut tree.

'Opposite it the track begins that takes you to Son Ponce. You'll pass some other houses, but Son Ponce is where the track ends.'

'Shouldn't I have the key?'

'The door will be open. Nobody goes up there. Let's see if your taxi's come.' It was waiting in the square.

Grue was crossing the road from the ceramics works when a car came up and stopped beside him. A head leaned out. 'A lift perhaps you would like?' The English was spoken with a Mittel-European accent.

'Thanks,' said Grue, 'but that's my way,' and pointed to the *camino*.

'Then you must be Meestair Grue! Our friend Evans told

us to look out for you. I am Baron Sloma. Permit me to present my wife, the Baroness. It is Son Ponce that you seek, is it not? More easy from above it is to arrive there. Permit us to carry you up the hill and I shall expose myself.' He reached back to open the rear door.

Grue got in. A Baroness who resembled his Chief Constable was not to be denied, though the lip between the teeth and promising moustache was predatory rather than just stiff. 'Good afternoon t'you, Baroness. You're very kind, Baron.'

After half a mile the road levelled out. The Baron stopped and pointed. 'There is it, Son Ponce, the house with the red tiles. That bigger one across the valley is for farmers, a convent once it was. You may walk agreeably through the trees and quite soon a path. Always you will see the house for farmers on your right.'

As Grue opened the door to get out the Baroness cried 'Hoch! Is it possible that you play the bridge, Meestair Grue? One fourth we need for lunch tomorrow.'

'With our young English friend! Of course!' The Baron handed Grue a card. 'You will lunch with us then, Meestair Grue. Much we anticipate our little game.'

Grue stood waving as the car went on up the hill and wondered at such ready hospitality. Then, marking his direction, he slid down the embankment and entered the wood, walking softly on pine needles. Already the red-tiled roof was hidden but the farmhouse remained in view. He came to a path and followed it.

Quite suddenly the house appeared through the trees and the path brought him to a terrace below it. A steep track wound downhill. The door was shut, so Grue took up a stone and rapped. The house was silent. He called out, and his voice dropped into the silence of the hillside.

Along the terrace a huge prickly-pear cactus leaned on a little hut. Beyond it someone had been smashing bricks. He

131

ducked under cactus leaves to look into the hut. It was a lavatory, an earth closet without a door. Flies rose up from the pit.

The hut faced a window with wooden shutters. Grue slid a knife between them and found the catch. As he swung the shutters back something scuttled in the dark interior. He stepped over on to a tiled ledge and down on to an earthen floor. There was a candle on the ledge. He lit it and looked around.

Broken laths hung from the ceiling, crumbling plaster. There were a few broken chairs, made of cane. He went through a doorway into what would be the kitchen, with a cement sink, clay dishes and a gas cooker. In a corner a chain hung from a windlass, a well. He pushed back the wooden cover and leaned over. Darkness. Beside the cooker there was a gas bottle. He switched it on and it hissed. As he opened the oven door, a long grey tail twitched and withdrew into the compartment below the burners.

At the other end of the main room was a staircase of black wood. Half way up, he found a room with a bath, a basin, a lavatory, all propped on supports of brick but with no connection for inflow or drainage, and an old wooden-framed camp bed.

Further up the stairs was a doorless opening into a long, low room, a sort of granary. Light streamed through the broken tiles on to a plaster floor which heaved and sagged and was penetrated with holes. At the far end a rat idly scratched its stomach.

Back downstairs he looked more carefully. There could be gold or half a dozen bodies under that earthen floor. Down the well there could be anything. He pushed the front door open till it grated to a halt on the flagstones outside. The light was fading. And something else was changing. There was a sound of bells. Grue stood in the

132

doorway listening. The sound was coming nearer, merging into something different, threatening. Grue stepped back as sheep rushed toward him with a clash of bells and thud of hooves. When they had passed he stepped out into a cloud of dust.

A small boy was sitting on a granite boulder at the corner of the house. Beside him there was a great black dog, its eyes red in the half-light. '*Pas bouger,*' said the child. From higher up the hill a bird called '*Tonk.*' In lower tone another answered, '*Tonk.*' The child's head turned. '*Houlette.*'

Round the corner came a stout man, stepping carefully. He motioned Grue into the house, then added brusquely, '*Allez!*'

In the main room Grue relit the candle. He propped a chair against one wall and sat on it with care. The stout man took one too and they considered one another across the earthen floor. The stout man had a heavy face, with a thin moustache. A Marseille gangster, Grue decided, not one of the hired help. '*Anglais?*' he asked. Grue nodded.

Outside there was the sound of hooves but muffled, more deliberate. Harness jingled and voices spoke quietly. Someone else came in. 'Who's he?' He had the sort of boot face that Grue always wanted to hit with an iron bar – but the bar would bend on this one.

'Is it all done?' the stout man asked.

'All done.' The boot face stared at Grue. 'So who are you?'

A little nervousness would suit his part. Grue stammered an explanation of his interest in buying the house. 'Evans!' exclaimed the gangster. 'What's Evans up to? Search this fellow!'

Boot face moved toward Grue. 'Stand up!' But a whistle broke the silence outside.

The Marseille gangster's head jerked round. '*Merde*!' There were three more whistles. 'Go!' said the gangster, and brought out a gun.

Boot face ran but was back almost at once. '*Guardia*!'

The gangster lumbered to his feet. 'Bring him. We must know what Evans is after.'

They pushed Grue out, the gun prodding at his back. It was time for him to make a move. He stumbled, brought an elbow round against the gun, and dropped and rolled. Above him something whanged against the wall. From higher up there was a *snap* and the Englishman cried out. Grue rolled again and, crouching, ran along the lower terrace. His former captors were running too. Again that *snap* and something whizzed through leaves. Grue stopped amongst olive trees, listening. Hooves moved quietly away.

Cautiously, from tree to tree, Grue went down the hillside until he could see the track. Two uniformed figures were pacing up it, rifles slung on shoulders. Light reflected from brass and patent leather. Spanish police. As they turned the next corner Grue slid on to the track and followed it down to the road below, the *camino*. There was the walnut tree. Somewhere a dog was yapping. Grue walked along the *camino* at a steady pace, meeting no one all the way. Loud voices were coming from the bar on the other side of the main road. He passed through the rectangle of light from the open door without being seen.

Back in his hotel Grue ordered beer and pondered. For sure that was a catapult that he had heard. He pondered further on hospitality and on smuggling and on gold. I'm a careful person, he reminded himself, and asked for a list of hotel telephone numbers.

'Not here,' they answered, 'no, not here,' until he got a

positive reply at the Hotel Mirador. 'Yes, Baron, Señor Potter is resident here.'

'His room, room twenty-two is it not? Of course, room fifteen. Put me through to him if you please.'

'Potter speaking,' said a voice he knew.

'*Ach! Hoch! Donner und Blitzen!*' Grue cried in German recalled from films and novels. '*Alle Männer-verlassen das Schiff!*' He was overdoing it. He was carried away by the drama of the situation and by too many beers drunk on an empty stomach. 'Ist the Baron who sprach. Ein ozzer freund we haffen who komm to play ze bridge. Always you still komm, nein?'

'Certainly, Baron, I have not forgotten.'

'Goot, goot, goot! Wunderbarischleik! So gutennacht-gaun, Herr Potter!' Grue looked at his watch. Eight o'clock – there would be time for a shower and a sandwich; they dined late in Spain.

Settled in a bar across the street, Grue ate tapas while he watched the window of Potter's hotel dining room. When Potter appeared he crossed the street and went straight upstairs. He had previously noted that the receptionist was cocooned in his own thoughts in the Spanish way, oblivious of all else. Grue picked the lock of room 15. The lock of Potter's case yielded to his art as readily. Inside were a catapult, the Dreerie story and two gold ingots. Grue locked up behind him and went down to the dining room.

Potter sat back, astonished, but still chewing, as Grue sat down and waved the waiter over. 'Let's see.' Grue scanned the menu. 'I'll have the sole and the roast pork. And bring a bottle of Riscal red and one of Murrieta white.' He smiled at Potter. 'Gathering information is a habit of mine, Potter. That's how I know of these two wines. What's that you've got there? Pour it away or finish it and have some of mine. Red or white?'

'Red,' said Potter automatically. 'Ha!' He waved his fork. 'The Baron!'

'Just so. The Baron and his little game. Ah, here's my sole.' For a time Grue concentrated on his fish. 'That was good,' he said at last. 'I was needing something. Yes, the Baron. He's arranged his game of bridge to get us both out of the way so that they can search our rooms. And maybe when they've got us in his house they'll search us too.'

'Who are they? These two at Son Ponce were holding you at gun-point. And there were more of them behind the house.'

'They're smugglers. Smugglers and gangsters. And there's more than one gang. This thing is dangerous, Potter. I'm grateful for your intervention with the catapult. You're quite a warrior with beer mugs and I heard about your mine, but you're not warrior enough to deal with these people. Already three people have been killed, and that's not including Boyle.'

'But what is it that they're after?'

'It's not just a few gold ingots. By the way, the score is now two all.' Grue started on his pork.

'Two what?'

'Two ingots. I found two in France. Stay where you are. Yours are still upstairs in your case.'

Potter dropped back into his chair. 'Where did you find yours?'

'In France. It's a long story.'

'I found two others in France myself and then someone took them while I was sleeping.'

Grue looked up from his pork and a grin of delight spread over his face. 'In Loup-sur-Cuddé? It was! Did anyone ever tell you that you snore?'

'Then it was you . . .'

'It was me. I have them safely hidden.'

'What's it all about? I know that there was some basis of

136

truth in the story of the Treasure of Tahag, for those stones we found under the floor were rubies and emeralds – "not of the very best quality", as the Armenian said – but they fetched a fair price when I sold them in London.'

'So they weren't just for the catapult? You have a brain, Potter, and I need it, and you need me if you're going on with this thing, for you can't cope with these people on your own. The time has come for us to make an alliance.'

'What sort of alliance?'

Grue looked Potter straight in the eye. 'We split everything two ways. If it's only a matter of a few ingots after all, we split three ways and I hand in one part to the authorities and get the credit for it.

'I've never taken bribes,' Grue reflected, 'for that puts you in someone else's power. But this . . . this is something different. No-one knows who the gold belongs to. And I tell you, Potter, there's far more in it. There may be millions!'

Potter was balancing chance and danger. There really was no choice. He remembered sliding down that rope and shuddered. 'What I got for the stones, that's mine?'

Grue waved a generous hand. 'That's yours. And you can have any manuscripts that turn up. Well, is it a deal?'

'It's a deal.' Potter reached out a hand and they shook on it. 'So what do we do next?'

'We exchange information. I'll tell you all I've been doing and you'll tell me all you know. Let's have another bottle of that Riscal.'

Over the new bottle they recounted their experiences. 'So Brown was that chaplain, as I thought,' mused Potter, 'and he wasn't drowned in Alexandria or Tangier. He brought his loot from Indonesia to Egypt, and got some at least back to England. But what's the truth about the Treasure of Tahag? And how do the smugglers come into the story?'

'I don't know. But it's something really big. The import-

137

ant thing is that we work together, Potter. Your brains and some of my skills will get us there. Now we should exchange all the papers that we've got and read them through tonight. Tomorrow we'll compare notes.' Grue got to his feet. 'I'll go now and get what I have.'

He was soon back. 'Here. Now bring me everything you've got. We'll read it all carefully and sleep on it. Tomorrow we'll put the ingots somewhere safe.'

'Where can we hide them?'

'In Evans' garden. There's a pile of bricks and rubble down at the far end. Another couple of bricks will never be noticed.'

'Where are your two ingots?'

'Well hidden. Don't trouble yourself about them. Let's get on with our readings. We should make an early start tomorrow – shall we say eight o'clock for breakfast here?'

Though Grue was weary, professional habit would not let him rest until he had read through all Potter's papers, even the Dreerie story once again, though he knew now that it had only been bait to catch something bigger in Hubble's hiding place. What had Miss Pring's unwitting burglary discovered there? Her letters lacked detailed description. Maybe she should be approached again.

What Potter had found behind *The Monarch of the Glen* were the title deeds to Son Ponce, and that was interesting. It was Hubble who had been the owner, not Brown. Who was now the owner? Evans maybe, but there was no evidence of that.

The only other thing was the septic tank plan that had been under Potter's floor with the rest. The compartment that had been outlined in red had given Potter the idea of opening it up to find his ingots. Could more be hidden in some of these other compartments? If they found nothing else, maybe they should go back to Son Ponce and have a look. The number on the back of the plan must be a technical reference, but something about that number bothered Grue. He fell asleep thinking about it.

Potter was weary too, but he read through all Grue's papers. Hubble's story was a sequel to the Dreerie one, Brown and the Professor arriving at Trieste from Cyprus with manuscripts. Then Hubble. Why had Brown called the Professor by the name of Hubble in the Dreerie story? And who was the Professor anyway? And what had become of him? *Mod cons reds* suggested he had fooled the Russians. Was the telegram about 'dolores' from Evans, the estate agent here?

What had become of the Professor? Fraulein Büstj had gone to Loup and married Hubble, and she may well have pushed Dr Wettstein into the Danube. She certainly seemed to have been a nasty woman.

What manuscripts had Hubble fled with from Vienna? Leonardo? Columbus? How had he disposed of them and where were they now?

The last thing Potter looked at, already half asleep, was the picture postcard. He could see the path down which he had stumbled to the coast and again he remembered that slide down the rope. No question of it, he was better with Grue's support in this business. He turned the postcard over. *This is what you must remember.* And the telephone number. Something about that number . . . He fell asleep.

Grue had it in the morning when he woke. *There had been no telephone in that house!* Should he keep it to himself? A hand shaken, honour among thieves . . . besides he needed Potter's expertise about manuscripts.

He waved the septic tank plan as he approached Potter in the dining room. 'The number, it's a bank account!'

'I know,' said Potter and held up the postcard. 'It's the same number. It'll be one of those Swiss ones, a numbered account. How do these things operate, Grue?'

'Anyone who has the number can draw on the account.'

'But why wasn't Brown using it? Why was he plittering about hiding gold ingots in holes? And why didn't Hubble use it?'

'They can't have known which bank held the account. And neither do we. We'll find it, though, we'll find it somehow.'

'Nothing about a bank in any of these papers. How can we find it?'

'We may have to go to Switzerland, but first I think we should have another look at that house in Loup. Have you a good memory for figures?'

'Fair enough.'

'Then memorise the number and then we'll destroy the postcard and the plan. The number is what they're all after. That's what Boyle was after when he broke into your house. We must not let them get it.'

When Grue was sure that Potter knew the number, he flushed the postcard and the plan down the lavatory. 'That's done,' he said when he came back. 'Now we've to prepare ourselves for the bridge party at the Baron's. We must admit to knowing nothing. We'll carry the rest of our papers on us, and we'll hide the ingots in Evans' garden right away.'

There was no one in the lane outside Evans' house. Grue sat astride the wall and took the ingots as Potter passed them up, then moved cautiously toward the pile of rubble. He paused, hearing something being dragged across gravel. The gardener! He made a detour to see where the fellow was headed. But it was not the gardener – it was Evans

140

dragging a hosepipe. He pulled it along the side of the house to a shed at the back, coiled it neatly and hefted it up on to a wooden peg, leaning forward on his toes. It was done with practised ease like a groom putting up harness. He was dapper, clad in slacks and undershirt, hair well brushed and undisturbed despite the labour. Grue remembered then how when he had first seen Evans, he felt he had seen that figure before. Evans had been standing outside the railway station, feet astride, hat clasped over stomach – the precise angle from the entrance for a waiting chauffeur. A chauffeur-groom! Hence the signed photographs, the priority seats on planes. A chauffeur-groom in peacetime and the servant of some senior officer in wartime, he would be adept at going through private papers. And he must have had many opportunities to insinuate himself into the rackets that burgeoned at the end of the war.

Grue drew back and made his way through the orange trees to the rubbish pile, where he pushed the ingots under other rubble. Returning, he heard voices raised in argument and again made a detour. The Marseille gangster was confronting Evans with wildly waving arms. 'Trust? Pouff! I also will be, and my friends. And the other? The Columbus thing?'

'The sea has that. Hubble disposed of the papers. But it is of no consequence. We shall get the number from these two.'

They disappeared round the corner of the house, still arguing, but in lower tones so that Grue made out nothing more. He went directly down the steps into the lane. It was deserted.

Grue found Potter sitting in the bar with a glass of cognac, the only customer. It was the usual sort of bar with the usual rows of bottles and the usual things floating in dark sauces. 'So they're all in it,' he muttered when he had told Potter what he had heard, 'they're all in it, but not together.'

'Grue, they've thrown the Columbus manuscripts into the sea! I could . . . I could do murder!'

'There never were any, Potter. It was just a hoax, the same as the rest of the Dreerie story.'

'There *was* something. Jokes derive from real events. And I have the proof, those stones I sold in London.'

'We'd better go.' Grue waved the barman over. He stretched out a leg to reach into his pocket.

Potter sat slumped in dejection as Grue counted money on to the table. Abruptly he sat up. 'Wait!' He put his hand on the money. 'Is that the wench you told me about, the one who had Brown's child?'

Grue glanced round at Begonia, who had come through a door behind the bar. 'Yes, that's her.'

'Isn't it possible that she knows something?'

'If she did, Evans would have had it out of her long ago. Come on.'

'But Evans hasn't got anything. He may have overlooked what was under his nose.'

A child appeared beside them, yammering with a disagreeable croak. It put a sticky hand on Grue's trouser leg. '*Basketito*,' said Grue in a kindly voice and brushed the child away. 'Since I don't know any Spanish I invent words. All Spanish children seem to be spoilt little baskets.'

'I'm going to have a word with her.' Potter went over to the bar. Words were exchanged, glasses filled. Grue got up and walked over to lean against the door. Potter was taking his time and Potter was taking too many cognacs.

The child was clawing at his leg, yammering and croaking. From the bar counter Potter signalled, pointing urgently to the table where they had been sitting. Begonia sat down at it, and the barman was bringing glasses. Grue pushed the child aside and went to join them. 'Well?'

'She has papers. She wants money for them.'

Grue eyed her grimly. 'Tell her to let us see them.'

Potter spoke in Spanish. Begonia sipped cognac, looking at them in a calculating way. She nodded once or twice, then went back round the counter. '*Basketito*,' muttered Grue, wiping his trousers with his handkerchief. Begonia came back with paper in her hand. She clasped it to her breast, rubbing together the thumb and forefinger of the other hand.

Grue brought out a five-hundred-peseta note. Begonia waved a finger. With a grunt Grue substituted a thousand. Begonia gabbled. 'She wants five thousand,' Potter said.

'Five thousand for a bit of paper? Ridiculous!' Grue brought out four thousand more.

Begonia looked greedily at the money. She tore in two the paper that she held. She gabbled.

'She'll give us half for five thousand. If we want the rest we'll have to pay her more.'

'She's mad! Let's have a look though.' A cautious exchange was effected. Grue smoothed out the paper. A brief note said: *It was I who selected it but the Professor approved.*'

'We'll have to get the rest of it, Grue.' Potter was emptying his pockets. 'How much money have you?'

'Nothing but traveller's cheques and enough cash to pay for all your cognacs.'

Begonia eyed Potter's money with disdain and gabbled.

Suddenly the bar was silent. The music had been switched off. The barman's hand moved a cloth slowly round and round upon the counter. Potter looked at Grue. 'She says she wants gold.'

'Gold? Gold for a bit of paper?'

'She says Brown had gold.'

Begonia held her hand so that they could see the last line of writing and a name below it. 'It's German, Grue. Von something is the name. It could be a bank in Zürich.'

Begonia was raising and lowering her hand. She might have been conducting an orchestra. Grue's eyes narrowed. 'Ask her where she got this.'

Begonia spat out the words in answer to Potter's question. 'She stole it from Brown's Frenchwoman. That was the last time that she saw Brown. She's not making much sense except for her decided views on the morality and appearance of the Frenchwoman. Grue, I think we're going to have to give her an ingot. You said yourself that they wouldn't be easy to dispose of.'

'I certainly didn't think it would be as easy as this.' Grue grimaced. 'All right, she gets an ingot. But she'll have to come outside with us to get it.'

Potter gabbled and Begonia gabbled back. She spat words at the barman, who switched the music back on. Begonia shrieked at the child, who had been oddly silent, and the child began to howl as Begonia followed Grue and Potter out into the lane.

Grue put a hand on top of the wall. 'We're agreed then?'

'Agreed.' Potter stooped with hands clasped to give him a leg up.

Grue wriggled over and disappeared. Begonia put a hand tentatively on Potter's chest. Potter reached for the other hand, which held the paper. She giggled and drew back. Grue's head re-appeared, and then he got astride the wall and reached down with the ingot. Begonia held up the paper. Their hands inched toward one another. The exchange was made.

Begonia stood with the ingot in her hands as Grue dropped down, then placed it between her feet and, hopping awkwardly, removed her knickers and wrapped them round it. She scurried into the bar.

There was a taxi in the square. As soon as it had started off they examined the paper. 'It's a poem,' said Potter. 'Von Hofmannsthal was a poet.'

'We've given that woman a gold ingot for a poem by a bloody Kraut?'

'We'll have to get someone to translate it. Maybe there are Germans in the hotel.'

There were.

'It's very beautiful,' the lady said, and read it in German:

> Doch ein Schatten fällt von jenen Leben
> In die anderen Leben hinüber,
> Und die leichten sind an die schweren
> Wie an Luft und Erde gebunden.
>
> Ganz vergessner Völker Müdigkeiten
> Kann ich nicht abtun von meinen Lidern,
> Noch weghalten von der erschrockenen Seele
> Stummes Niederfallen ferner Sterne.

'It is a picture of one of the old ships of Greece or Rome, and across the slaves at oars fall the shadows of their cruel masters. Shall I write it for you in English?' She thought a little, then wrote:

> Yet a shadow falls from those lives
> On to the other lives,
> The light bound to the heavy
> As the air and the earth are bound together.
>
> The weariness of forgotten people
> I cannot hold away from my eyelids,
> Nor from my frightened soul
> The silent falling of distant stars.

145

They had been fortunate to find her for she was just setting off for the beach. 'Our German words are rather long,' she said as she gathered up her things, 'but our thoughts and memories are long too.'

'Nothing about a bank. Let's have another cognac.'

'You've had enough but I could do with one myself.'

Potter turned to call the waiter and there was Begonia at his side. 'More gold!' She held out paper.

No translation was required. Grue waved a hand. 'Tell her where the other ingot is. But she'll have to go for it herself.'

In Begonia's eyes were greed and innocence and worldly wisdom as she thought over what Potter said. Worldly wisdom won. She dropped the paper on the table and departed urgently in a taxi.

The paper, which was crumpled and smelled strongly of Begonia, said simply, *The poem is the method. No names, just the poem and the number.*

'Look! That woman swindled us! This was torn from the bit with the poem on it.'

'No matter. Now we know how to get money out of the account.'

'But we still don't know where the account is.' Grue ran his finger angrily along the torn edge. 'You know, this handwriting is Mrs Hubble's, same as in those letters. She kept this knowledge to herself. She had the poem and Hubble had the number. Who had the name of the bank?'

'Grue, I've been thinking. Those words you heard in Evans' garden – "The sea has them". It could be a capital C. That might mean the Capo of the Mafia. Maybe the manuscripts weren't thrown into the sea. Maybe they were handed over to the Capo. We could find out who he is from Evans or the Baron.'

'How are you going to do that? Beat them up?'

'They could be manuscripts unknown to scholars, Grue! We can't leave them to a gangster!'

'The gangsters will find us before we find them. Forget about the manuscripts and use your brain to find where the bank is! We'll have to go back to that house in Loup. It's where all these papers came from. We'd better make arrangements for getting out of here. I'll take a taxi to Palma and book seats on the plane to Marseille. We'll still have to go to the Baron's bridge party, to persuade them that we don't know anything. And I'll need money. We'll have to cash traveller's cheques.'

With that done Grue got into a taxi. 'Don't pack,' he said, 'but have everything ready for a quick departure.'

When Grue had gone, Potter went up to rearrange his luggage. The papers, the Dreerie and the rest? None of them mattered now, only what they had got from Begonia. He was looking at the poem when the phone rang. A Señor Evans wished to speak to him. About Son Ponce, he supposed.

'No hurry about that,' Evans said, 'though we could have a chat about it if you're free now and care to join me in the square. I'd like you to meet some of our expatriate community. They gather here for a drink about this time.'

Nothing to lose, maybe something to be gained. 'Delighted. Be with you shortly.'

Evans waved from a table when Potter came into the square. 'You like our cognac? They bring the bottle when they see me coming.' He pointed out celebrities. 'That's Crappage, he's a distinguished author as I expect you'll know. He's the man who took the lid off Wimbledon as that woman took the lid off Peyton Place. The fellow with him, the one with the diamond earrings, is his publisher – Smat Books.'

Potter made idle remarks about Son Ponce, listening to the bearded conversation.

'No,' said the publisher. 'That won't do. You won't get Primitive Methodists burning your book in Bootle.'

'The Scotch?'

'No,' said the publisher. 'That won't do. They won't read a book that's not been written by a Scotchman.'

'Women?'

'No,' said the publisher. 'That won't do. They're all too busy writing books themselves.'

'China? There's a lot of Chinamen.'

'No,' said the publisher. 'That won't do. Inscrutable.'

'Footballers?'

'It's an idea.' The publisher considered. 'Football fans buy all the Sunday papers to see which says most about their team.' He did rapid sums. 'All the papers, that's near enough the price of a Smat book. I think you've got it! And football fans might pay for your assassination.'

Potter turned back to the merits of Son Ponce. 'I'll need more time to think about it. Talking of which, I can't stay long. I'm expected for lunch at Baron Sloma's. You'll know him, I expect.'

'Indeed I do! The Baron is the doyen of our expatriate community, comes of a very old family. And here he comes, the Baron himself! And the Baroness too! How delightful!' Evans pushed chairs about.

'Talk of the devil,' Potter said. 'I was just this moment telling Mr Evans of your invitation. He was not at all surprised.'

But Evans was not listening. 'What's she doing with him?' he muttered, staring across the square. The Marseille gangster was in close conversation with Begonia. His dog was tied to the railings of the bandstand and the small boy, its guardian, sat on a nearby step.

The square was noisy in many tongues. Potter's attention

148

was taken by two rather precious youths who were discussing art galleries at the next table. They had that curious movement of mouth that Australians have, as if they'd eaten something sour.

'The Uffizi,' murmured one of the Australians.

'Van der Goes,' breathed the other.

'That little patch of yellow co'n.'

'Up in the left hand co'ner.'

'Hits you for six. Like fleece.'

Observing Potter's interest, the Baron called them over. 'You bin to Aussie?' enquired one when the chairs had been reshuffled. 'You should see it. Sheep! You should see them.' He stretched his arms out. 'Big!'

'Vot ees zes sheep?' enquired the Baroness.

'Ees animal,' explained the Baron. 'Hass four laigs in every corner.'

'Perhaps you do not half them in your country, Baroness,' slurred Potter. 'They drink a lot of wasser and perhaps in your country there isn't any wasser . . . water.' He poured himself some more brandy and addressed himself to the problem. 'Wet countries suit them besser. It's like haffing to go out of Wales to get a drink on Sundays. But they must wash in Wales. How do they wash when there isn't any washer?' He stuck out his arms and legs and waggled all four limbs.

The Baroness regarded Potter's motions with suspicion. 'Vot you say about my countree?'

'Big,' said one of the Australians.

'Fleece,' said the other.

'Aha!' exclaimed the Baroness. 'Like had Columbus. Admirable sheeps. In Saxe-Coburg, my countree, are many sheeps.'

'Top hole!'

'Hits you for six!'

'Like Van der Goes!'

'In Marseille anyzing goes. All interesting sax.' The sweating face of the Marseille gangster intruded. 'Co-bugger and sheep I will arrange.'

The author and the publisher leaned closer.

'And ze goat I pleasure for you, all top hole. Ze donkey also,' he remembered.

When Potter tried to recall later what had been said, he had only a confused memory but he was sure that the Australians claimed that Columbus had discovered Australia. 'That's why we're called colonials,' he said. 'Columbus was a top-hole buzza.'

'I didn't understand it all though,' Potter told Grue. 'I think that they were drunk.'

What Grue quickly understood when he joined the party in the square was that Potter was decidedly drunk. 'Remember we're to play bridge,' he muttered.

'Ze bridge of ze Baron, yes.' The Marseille gangster was watching closely. 'And Monsieur interests himself in the sheep of Son Ponce.'

'To ze bridge, Baron!' cried the Baroness, and they followed in her wake.

'How much better we would all understand one another if we all spoke different languages,' Potter mumbled as Grue steered him toward the Slomas' car. 'The more you understand what people say, the less you understand them. If no one understood anyone else, there would be no occasion for misunderstanding. Do you understand what I mean, Grue?'

The Baron's house was imposing and the room they were ushered into was opulent. Light fell softly on richly coloured carpets and shone on fine porcelain. Before a wide fireplace a table was set for cards. Another table was laden with all sorts of delightful things to eat and drink, and maid rolled in a trolley bearing more. 'One helps oneself while playing,' said the Baroness.

Potter excused himself and, while they waited, Grue strolled round the room admiring everything. The Slomas fussed with drinks and cards.

When Potter came back he was a little pale but steadier on his feet. They cut for deal. Not for partners, said the Baron. Only with himself would the Baroness play. 'But now, let us have a small stake, more interesting is it. A hundred, five hundred?' They settled on a hundred.

The visitors did well in the first rubber. They were making more of their cards than their hosts. The Baron was given to rash plunges and the Baroness was erratic. As the score was totted up, the two Australians slipped in and drew up chairs on opposite sides of the table. Though properly silent during the play, they both twitched restlessly.

Things turned in favour of the hosts. They quickly won two rubbers and insisted that the stakes be raised. 'Five hundred will be more exiting,' declared the Baroness. At this point the Marseille gangster lumbered in and sat brooding by the telephone while his dog explored the room.

After another victory for the hosts Grue suggested that the next rubber be the last. The Baron consulted his watch. 'One more should do.'

Potter opened with a bid of three no trumps and, this being unchallenged, 'I'm going to stretch my legs,' said Grue. The Baron exchanged a meaningful look with the Marseille gangster as Grue strolled to the door. He was carrying a large envelope.

When Grue returned, Potter had made his contract with an overtrick. The cards were dealt again. The Baroness made the final bid, four hearts. The Australians twitched. The Baroness made four hearts exactly. One more game for rubber.

The Baron showed considerable excitement as he sorted

out the cards he had been dealt. The bidding swept up to a small slam in spades bid by the Baron. Potter doubled. The Baron redoubled.

The Baron had gathered in the first two tricks when the telephone rang. The Marseille gangster hooked up the receiver, scowled, and gave it to the Baroness, who had jumped up from the table. The Baron paused to listen. 'Ha! Ja! Nozzings?' The Baroness frowned.

'Nozzings?' called the Baron. 'Nozzings?' He put down his cards and went to take the receiver. 'Nozzings?'

The telephone crackled.

'Not?'

The telephone sighed.

The Baron and the telephone exchanged dejected looks. He put down the receiver slowly and returned to the table. Absently he picked up his cards.

While the telephone conversation had been going on Grue had been watching with curiosity the movements of a large blancmange which stood in virgin whiteness on the trolley's lower shelf. It had begun to quiver and sway. It wobbled. It bellied out voluptuously, retreated coyly, bellied out again. Grue went over to pick up a biscuit and to investigate the causes of this exotic dance. On the farther side of the trolley was the Marseille gangster's dog, licking with a long red tongue and appreciative slurps. 'Clever doggie,' murmured Grue, reaching out a hand. The dog bared possessive teeth.

When the game resumed, the Baron appeared to be distracted, fingering one card, touching another, looking in a puzzled way at the Australians. They twitched. The Baron hesitated one more moment and then he plunged. He played the ace of diamonds from dummy, trumped it from his own hand, then led the king of diamonds. 'I fear you have revoked,' said Potter.

Not only had the Baron revoked but in the same masterly

stroke he had trumped his own ace and destroyed his last entry to dummy, where master tricks lay in profusion.

The Baron cursed and flung down his hand.

'So all the rest are ours.' Grue smiled benignly. 'Doubled, redoubled, vulnerable. Shall we settle for fifty thousand? Tidier without the odd hundred.'

For the first time the Marseille gangster showed interest in the game. He put a large square thumb on the score sheet. '*Caramba! Sacrébleu! Nom d'un chien!*'

'Your doggie's name is quite a mouthful.' Potter got his wallet out and looked expectantly at the Baron. But it was the Marseille gangster who paid, the Baron having made no motion. 'It is of honour,' said the gangster. 'I settle vis ze Baron when we settle also the telephone account. But now I take you to San Baccho in my car. And do not forget that envelope.'

'Envelope?' Grue was looking at his watch. 'Here, hold it for me while I show Potter something. Come and look at this carpet, Potter. I do believe it's Isfahan.' He drew Potter into an alcove. 'Get down and look at it closely, Potter, all these knots and stitches. Get down, Potter, there's going to be a bang!'

With Grue's hand upon the back of his neck, Potter's face was inches from the carpet when the bang went off. 'Right on time!' cried Grue when things had stopped flying round the room. 'Let's go!'

The room was in a mess. The trolley had disintegrated, the delicacies it had borne were plastered round the walls and on the ceiling. The dog lay bleeding from what had been its head.

Tumbled in a heap, the Baron, the Baroness and the Australians twitched and groaned. The Marseille gangster waved a feeble hand as Grue retrieved his envelope and took from him car keys and a gun. Grue raised the gun as the gangster's boot-faced friend ran in and, whirling him by

153

one arm, he whacked him on the side of the head. Then he slashed at telephone wires with the knife boot-face had dropped. Potter was in a car before he knew it. Grue fiddled with something at the back, then he was at the wheel and they were swerving through the gates.

'What happened?'

'Explosive charge with a timing device. Very neat. I put it in the blancmange.'

'I hope they're not seriously hurt.'

'Maybe. Probably not.' They were hurtling down the road to San Baccho. 'They'd have hurt us more.' Grue glanced in the mirror. 'I fixed explosives to all the cars. Found them in the cellar of the house in Loup.

When we get to the hotel, pay the bill and bring your stuff quickly. Don't wait for change. And don't look for papers. I brought them all myself.'

After brief stops at both hotels, Grue drove on at speed to Palma. 'Not much time to spare. We'll make it though.' He glanced at Potter. 'Still game to go back to the house in Loup?'

'We must.' Potter had got over the shock of the explosion. After all he had set one off himself. 'I still have the key. I wonder how Brown got hold of that.'

'Theft, bribery.' Grue concentrated on the road.

They were in good time for the plane and nobody attempted to stop them boarding it. 'Do you think they'll be waiting for us in Marseille?' Potter worried.

'Not at the airport. At the railway station maybe – it would suit them better.' Grue passed over the envelope with the papers. 'Here! Go through these again. There may be something that we've missed and it'll take your mind off reception committees. There's one I never understood – that telegram about Dolores. Were they in the white-slave trade as well? The Marseille gangster would be the one for that. And Evans, Evans is a Welsh name, and they do say

154

that the Welsh have a genius for religion, music and sex – though not necessarily in that order. Why did he call himself Punto? Sort of nickname, do you think? I suppose he would be above nicknames now he's so respectable.'

Potter cackled. 'The telegram's about money. It's dollars – not Dolores. And *punto* just means stop as it's used in telegrams.' Still cackling, Potter settled to his reading.

Grue was silent, thinking his own thoughts. Something about Dolores . . . *renovare Dolores*. Why should the Latin they had beaten into him at grammar school come back now? *Quack quicksy miserrima vidi.* That was someone called Pious . . . Not a Pope, it was that fellow who founded the Roman empire . . . Aeneas, Pious Aeneas. He abandoned some woman and sailed over this blue sea. It must have been the sea that brought back the words. He began to whistle *The girl I left behind me.*

Potter finished with the papers. 'Nothing.' He sat looking out at the sea. 'I've been thinking again about what you heard in Evans' garden. The words do suggest a capital C. It could be the Capo of the Mafia but there's another possibility. The house in Loup belongs to that Highland chieftain you met at Foovie. Wasn't he called Capocoolie or something like that? Could he be the Capo of the Mafia?'

'The Capercailzie? I don't see it. I didn't in fact meet him but I heard enough to discount the possibility of his being the Capo. I suppose he might know something, though. If he does, I have some leverage to get it out of him.' Grue recounted the story of the Capercailzie's stolen silver. 'So I'm pretty sure it's buried in Bawdy Raw.'

'We could phone him.'

'I suppose we could.'

'Curious, isn't it, that both your Chief Constable's silver and this Caper fellow's silver were stolen.'

'Not so curious when you think about it. The Capercailzie's ancestors were high-ranking gangsters who swindled and robbed their neighbours. Probably so were the Chief Constable's. That's how people get big houses and fill them up with silver. Look at the way the Great Train Robbers live on the Costa Plastica, and all that lot who have castles in the Dordogne. So if they are robbed in their turn, it's just like water finding its own level. 'So who has the right to what? I've sometimes wondered when I've had to arrest some yobbo who has stolen an old lady's teapot, how did she acquire the teapot in the first place? Who is guilty of what? In the end we're all guilty.'

'What is it that the poem says? The light are bound to the heavy as earth is bound to air. A shadow from those lives falls on the other lives. That woman in Vienna had seen both sides, her own lot strutting in victory and then the Russians getting their own back.'

'That print in your office says it too. Life's a struggle on muddy ground. Some get stuck in the scrum from the beginning and have to push and shove and have their ears pulled off while others, who've been put in the three-quarter line, wait elegantly for the ball to drop into their hands. What I can't stand is the smugness of people who start with all the advantages, and the peevish resentment of the losers is as bad if they just accept defeat. Myself,' said Grue, 'I don't accept it.'

There was no sign of a reception committee at Marseille airport. 'There should be a bus.' Grue looked round.

'There's one.' Potter lifted his case. 'No, it's for Aix. Look, why don't we go there for a night? I don't fancy hanging around Marseille railway station and we've done enough today.'

'Is it far?'

'No farther than Marseille station.'

'Let's do that then.'

In the half-hour's journey Grue thought about the Capercailzie. He might know something. Besides, if no more came out of this whole venture than a couple of ingots, he might as well go back to his job with credit for finding someone's silver. 'What you said about the Capercailzie,' he said as they got off the bus, 'it makes sense. We'll phone him.'

Enquiries found the number listed for Victor Grummle, Foovie Castle. The call went through promptly and Grue knew the bleat at the other end.

'My name is Grue, sir, Inspector Grue of the Loocestershire police. Should I address you as Capercailzie?'

'If you wish, Mr Grue, if you wish. No, no, Deirdre, don't put it there. In what way can I help you, Mr Grue? Inspector, I think you said?'

'I am phoning because I think I can help you in the matter of your stolen silver.'

'Good heavens! You've found it! But how did it get to France?'

'It's not here, Capercailzie, but I think I do know where it is, and, if you answer a couple of questions, I should be able to put you in the way to get it back.'

'Anthea, stop that this minute! Nanny! Nanny! Do come and take the children out of the kitchen! I have an important call from France. Inspector Grue, I remember now, weren't you in Foovie at the time of the burglary? Grant, our constable thought you were the burglar.'

'There was some misunderstanding, sir. Now a couple of questions. Are you –'

'Oh there you are, Nanny! Just look what the children have been doing! What was it you wanted to know, Inspector?'

'Are you a writer, Capercailzie?'

'A writer? One of these lawyer fellows who charge so much for doing nothing? Certainly not.'

'That's not what I meant, sir. Do you write fiction?'

'Good gracious, no! What would I do that for?'

'You own a house near Nice, Capercailzie. Have you ever seen written stories there?'

'Oh yes. The butler wrote them.'

'The butler? Will I find him there?'

'No. He's dead, poor fellow. Fell down the stairs and broke his neck.'

'If I went to the house, sir, whom would I find there?'

'Business people. I leased it to them.'

'Do you think I might look for papers in the house?'

'I don't really know. I haven't been there in years. Last I heard of it was from the butler's daughter. She came to live in Foovie after her mother's death.'

'That was Miss Hubble?'

'That's right. Hubble was the butler.'

'And her mother died?'

'Yes. She broke her neck too. Fell from the village wall. But if it's a story you're looking for, I have one here. Hubble sent it shortly before his death. For some reason he asked me to keep it in a safe place. It's in the library.'

Grue spoke very carefully. 'Capercailzie, will you please go and find that story? Will you go now and find it and phone me back?' Grue gave the number and laid down the receiver.

They waited in their room, and had a pot of tea sent up. It was two hours before the call came. 'Inspector Grue? I've found it. It wasn't in the library. Nanny had it. She was going to read it to the children but decided it was unsuitable and then forgot to put it back. They've been reading a story called *Patient Place* instead.'

'Capercailzie, what is the story about?'

'A fish, I suppose. The children do like animal stories. They must have read *Salar the Salmon* half a dozen times.'

'Not that one. The other, the one the butler sent.'

158

'I don't really know. I haven't read it. Wait. It seems to be about Christopher Columbus.' There was a sound of paper rustling. 'That's right, Columbus.'

Grue breathed deeply. 'Capercailzie, sir, will you send me that story? Not the one about the flounder, the Columbus one. Will you send it by the quickest means you can?'

'Of course, my dear fellow. I'll get it to the post right away. Where do I send it to?'

'Send it . . . send it to me at this hotel. And now I'll tell you where to find your silver . . . But don't dig up the larger hole.'

'It won't be the original manuscripts,' ruminated Potter over coffee and croissants in the Cours Mirabeau next morning, 'but copies will be almost as important.'

'Bugger that, it's the name of the bank we want. He must have put it in the story.'

'I hope it comes soon. We're running out of money.'

'Yes, there's the hotel bill, and we'll have to buy rail tickets to Zürich. And we'd better pay for protection here. I'll go and collect the ingots that I hid at Loup and sell them.'

'Won't that be difficult?'

'I'll do it through the vice squad. We won't get anything like their real value but it should be enough.'

Grue left Potter alone for a day. He was evasive when he returned but he had his wallet filled with francs. 'Satisfactory. Best you don't know the details – it's a matter of professional etiquette. Anyway, we have the assurance of protection both from the police and from the Mafia.'

Three days passed and nothing came, and then the Capercailzie phoned again. 'Not got it yet? I sent it off directly. I've sent another envelope too. But the great news is that I found my silver exactly where you said it would be. I can't tell you how grateful I am. But it was about this other envelope I'm phoning. It came some time ago with a letter from a lawyer in Loup asking me to see that it was delivered to Miss Hubble and I quite forgot about it while she was here. Now she's disappeared I thought it best to open it. It's not important, something about a septic tank. You'll be able to find her address more easily than I can. I hope the story is all there. I'm afraid the children had been playing with some of the pages. Paper darts, I think.'

The story came the following day. They opened the envelope once they had ordered coffee and croissants at their favourite café.

The Columbus Manuscripts

As the 500th anniversary of Columbus' historic voyage approaches, already there are cackling academics scratching over old ground with one eye fixed on the enormity of his discovery, the other cocked in the direction of some comfortable perch from which their own discoveries may be proclaimed. Behind well-feathered tails, kicked carelessly aside, lost under a detritus of academic droppings, lie the assured words of the Great Discoverer himself: 'For my voyage to the Indies I had no help from reason, mathematics, or maps of the world. It was but a fulfilment of what had been foretold by the prophet Isaiah.'

The documents which have come into my possession confirm the prophecy. It was not just a mistake that anyone going that way might have made: only Columbus could have discovered America.

How came these documents to be gathered together? And why were they buried in the deepest, darkest file of the Archive of the Indies? By whose instructions? We shall never know. Sufficient that they have passed from the unscrupulous hands that snatched them and into the secure ones of a responsible scholar.

I have abridged what is told of Columbus' early years. Not everyone will wish to follow the tedious tale of how he abandoned ship in Venice, of his garbling the gibberings of Savonarola in those lectures in philosophy which were to charm the harem of the Bey of Algiers, of his letting go the ladder whilst bowing to the Pope so that a passing bishop was prematurely promoted Cardinal by staggering Leonardo's paint-pot. A glimpse of his boyhood in his father's weaving workshop in Genoa will suffice.

> Shuffle, shuffle, snock.
> Shuffle, shuffle, snock.
> Snick, snock, snuck . . .

Snafu! Christopher had got it wrong again. 'I wanna be a diplomat!' he snuffled.

'The very thing!' the weaver woofed, making strange comparison between Christopher's knowledge of his fundamentals and his inappropriate use of his elbow. So Christopher was sent to sea to learn a trade.

He never did quite get the hang of things on shipboard. Sails and spars and cordage were just like his father's weaving machines back there in Genoa. But the captain found employment for him in the galley and there he was a fair success, having long fingers well suited to combing out spaghetti.

Christopher was long in everything. It was this longitude and the latitude he permitted himself in claims of his experience that would persuade the Queen of Spain to make him her admiral.

'This is appalling, Grue!'

'There must be something in it.'

'But there's nothing here that could have come from genuine manuscripts.'

'It's not old scratchings that we're looking for. Read a bit more.'

The agent of police and the delegate of Mafia exchanged shrugs. The Englishmen seemed upset. *Il y aura du grabuge.*

Christopher first floats into the light of hitherto known history on the shore of Portugal, sole survivor of a ship lost at sea. It can now be told that there was another survivor. To the spar by which Christopher was saved clung also O'Hooligan, a marvellous growth of whiskers with a fine tenor voice but no other material substance. It was O'Hooligan who, with Bisningham and Toscanelli, set Christopher on course. Toscanelli was a Florentine philosopher, a Capo of the Mafia and President of Florence FC. He was in Lisbon to lecture at the English Cultural Centre. As the sage approached the splendid entrance of Lisbon's most prestigious hotel he was saluted by a tall figure. Whiskers stooped attentively over his luggage. 'Admirable!' cried Toscanelli, observing how the hotel fronted on the sea. He loathed the sea, had loathed it since his crossing from Sicily to the mainland.

'Admiral?' The tall figure caught sight of itself in the glass of the hotel door. 'Why not?' It teased out epaulettes.

Toscanelli was looking forward to his lunch. He had arranged for a rival to be drowned in view of the dining room.

For the purposes of his lecture Toscanelli had a map. It had been drawn for him by the small boy who was normally his companion on long voyages overland

162

but the child now had mumps. The map showed that East is West, so that if you started off from an imaginary island you would certainly meet yourself somewhere, coming or going, on a journey round the world. Toscanelli had this map in a briefcase, one of those then fashionable.

Bisningham too had a map. In an identical briefcase. Bisningham's map had been drawn by Cardinal d'Ailly to amuse his grandchildren. It demonstrated that if a man walked 20 miles a day he would go round the world in 4 years, 16 months and 3 days, always provided that he was prepared to walk on water. Bisningham had borrowed the map from the Cardinal, who was a director of the company, to use at a conference of sales staff. Sales had been slipping.

Bisningham was staying at the same prestigious hotel as Toscanelli, but lunch was not on the expense account. Hurrying out of the hotel, headed for the Fried Chicken, Bisningham held his briefcase before his face to prevent recognition by anyone of consequence. There was bound to be a collision. Of such events is history made.

Some years after these events a tall figure bowed low before the King of Portugal and reached through whiskers to produce two maps in support of his claims to be made Admiral of the Ocean Sea, a knight with golden spurs and President of America. Hitherto history records the opinion of the King: 'A big talker, boastful in setting forth his accomplishments, full of fancy.' The King came to a decision, as can now be revealed: 'Let him be President.'

The Bishop of Ceuta, who was in attendance, observed, hitherto history tells us, that the tall figure's claims were 'simply founded on imagination'. What the

Bishop's advice was can now be told: 'He is a liar to boot.'

So Columbus moved to Spain.

'It's rubbish, Grue, all rubbish!'

'Pull yourself together, Potter. There must be something in it. Why else did Hubble want it to be kept in a safe place? We'll read the rest in our hotel room.'

The agent of police and the delegate of Mafia fell into step and followed them to their hotel. They pressed agile ears against the room door but could make nothing of the muttered words and so retired to a bar from which the entrance of the hotel could be observed. Consequently they missed Grue's triumphant cry: 'We have it, Potter, we have it all! Danton et Cie are the bankers! And look, the account number's here as well! It's the date of Columbus setting sail – third day of the eighth month and 1492 the year – 381492!'

They missed, too, the agent and the delegate, a telephone conversation between Grue and a Swiss banker.

'Nine? Nine million? . . . Oh, nine thousand? . . . Nine hundred! There must be some mistake . . . No, no, I understand. The bank does not make mistakes. But are you quite sure? Nine hundred Swiss francs?'

There was a further conversation that the agent and the delegate missed and it will not be reported here. All that the agent and the delegate had to report that day was that the Englishmen remained shut in their room but for excursions to a shop that sold wines and spirits.

Next morning they appeared and drank much strong coffee. Then they opened a letter, speaking without flattery of its sender, and suddenly all was changed. They uttered cries, waved their arms and rushed precipitately back to their hotel. Again the agent and the delegate applied their agile ears to the room door but, nothing being clear to them, they retired to watch from the convenient bar. It was thus that they missed the formulation of a plan.

'It must be millions, Grue! Pounds, not Swiss francs!'

'Near enough ten million, I reckon.'

'Read it again, Grue, my glasses are all misted up.'

'All right. I'll leave out the endearments. He says he wrote the Columbus Manuscripts and sent them to the Capercailzie to be put in a safe place, reckoning that that was just what the Capercailzie wouldn't do, so that someone would get hold of them and they would all start fighting and be thoroughly bamboozled. Cunning old devil!'

'Even if it was Hubble who wrote the Columbus Manuscripts, there's some authentic history in them. They must have had some genuine documents that they took to Vienna. Hubble didn't invent it all.'

'Forget it, Potter. Whatever they did have, you'll never find it now.'

Potter sighed deeply. 'Go on then.'

'Hubble and Brown had been left on a boat laden with gold ingots and brandy whilst the rest of them were arguing in a bar. Brown slipped the moorings and took the boat out to sea. He sailed it round to a cove where there was a private jetty owned by a writer called Henry Tombs. Brown intended to take on food and water for a long voyage, and maybe fuel for the boat, but no sooner had they tied up than a group of young fellows and girls poured aboard. There were a lot of them who used to live at Tombs' expense – sculptors, poets and painters is what they called themselves. They danced about, discovered a case of brandy and started in on it. And then carried Brown off with them. And another case of brandy. Really carried. He was shouting and struggling to get free. Hubble they ignored. He would be too fuddy-duddy for them.

'Hubble waited a while. Then he thought he would go home to Son Ponce. Then he thought again and began to unload the gold. He does go on a bit. He started with a couple of ingots and hid them in between rocks in a place concealed by bushes. He waited then, but still Brown didn't return. So he unloaded some more ingots. And then some more. And then he just went on and unloaded them all. It was a lot of work, he says. There were about a thousand.

'And then he began to wonder what the smugglers would do when they found the boat and no gold or Brown. So he decided he'd better sink the boat. He opened a bottle of brandy and started the engine. That took a bit of time because he didn't know anything about engines. And he had to find out how to make the boat go backwards. When he'd done that, and unmoored it, and got it going out to sea, he started to pull levers and turn wheels that might make the boat sink. He jumped overboard when he was sure it was going in the right direction, swam ashore and went home.

'When the smugglers asked what had happened, he said that Brown had thrown him overboard. They believed him. They didn't think he was very bright. But he was. He began to take the ingots up to Son Ponce, only a few at a time. What he did with them I'll read in his own words.

'"It was at this time I had been building a septic tank. I went at it now with renewed vigour, using gold ingots instead of bricks. There were so many that I filled up some of the compartments with ingots and that's why it never worked.

'"Brown disappeared. He would be scared of the others, and rightly so. Although they believed my story they were quite unpleasant and I was glad to leave Son Ponce when the Capercailzie offered me a job as butler. Brown did go back later. What he told them I don't know. I think he persuaded them that I had taken the gold to France. That's what he thought himself. Anyway, they were all watching me and Brown. Once my house in Loup was burgled and my papers stolen.

166

' "Your mother knows that I hold the secret of some hidden wealth and as long as I keep the secret I am safe. If she ever finds what it is, I would fear for my life. She is a ruthless woman." '

'And so was her daughter,' Grue mused. 'I think the mother pushed the old man down the stairs and then the daughter pushed her mother over the parapet where you climbed down.'

'Poor old Hubble. There's one argument in favour of hanging, Grue. If they bring it back they'll have to appoint a hangperson as well as a hangman and they'll have to hang as many women as men. Women's rights demands as much.'

'You can write to Women's Lib about it, Potter. In the meantime there are more important things to do. We must go to Zürich and draw out what there is in that account. We must go to Zürich and then disappear completely.'

The agent of police and the delegate of Mafia kept watch in turns all that day and through the night. What they had failed to observe was a drainpipe that offered easy descent from the Englishmen's room to a street behind the hotel. When they investigated in the morning they found the room deserted and all the luggage gone. We do not know what penalty they paid. The sea is not far off and holds its secrets.

Part 5

The Chief Constable Chews it Over

The Chief Constable was at breakfast when the phone call came. His daughter Daphne took the call. 'Daddy, there's a commissionaire on the phone for you.'

The Chief Constable laid down *Horse and Hound.* 'Ask him what he wants.'

'He's a policeman, Daddy. He's speaking from France.'

'What's a policeman doing in France?' Irritably the Chief Constable got up to take the phone himself. 'Good morning t'you. Colonel Rhonepipe-Doodle speaking.'

'*Bon jour, Monsieur. S'agit d'un agent de police perdu.*'

'Daphne, come and translate this. Why can't these foreigners speak English!'

Daphne took the receiver. '*Parlez-vous français, Mossoo?*' She listened to a torrent of explanation. 'A policeman *perdu?*'

'*Oui, oui. C'est pressant!*'

'He needs to go to the loo, Daddy, and he says he's in a hurry.'

'These foreigners have no self-control.' The Chief Constable's lip was stiff with disapproval. 'Ring off, Daphne.'

Obstinately the telephone rang again. 'Mees Rhonepipe-Doodle? *Tant pis, tant mieux!*'

'Daddy, it's that commissionaire again. He says his aunt has been to the loo as well and now she is feeling better.'

'But what is it that the fellow wants?'

169

Daphne returned the receiver to her ear. 'Two English-men in aches?'

'*Avec le sangfroid habituel des Anglais.*'

'With the usual bloody cold of the English.'

The telephone squawked on excitedly. 'One of them was called Grue and he was a policeman. It was remarked when he entered a fish at the hotel.'

'Grue? How could it be Grue? Grue's missing.'

'Wait, Daddy! While the door of entry was under obser-vation they descended their baggages behind and have disappeared without paying their hotel bill.'

The Chief Constable's swizzle-stick was waving wildly. 'I don't understand this at all. What has become of Grue? Ask the commissionaire if he suspects foul play!'

'*Mossoo, mon père demande de la possibilité d'un jeu avec poules* . . . Daddy, he's rung off!'

Some years afterwards the Chief Constable was taking tea with Inspector Tidd in the New World Olde Worlde Tea Shoppe. They had been lucky to get a table.

'Mrs Grue's done very well for herself since she came into that money,' ventured Tidd. 'This place must be a little gold mine with all these foreign visitors.'

'Foreigners?' The Chief Constable glanced round at neighbouring tables where a variety of clients filled the Tea Shoppe with hisses, grunts and gurgles. 'I had a lot of trouble with foreigners when Grue disappeared. There was a commissionaire who phoned from France, seems he was some sort of policeman too. They've all sorts over there.'

The waitress, Dilsie Creepin' Mouse, was at their table with more chocolate buns. She sneezed.

'Even worse in Italy they tell me, sell ice-cream on traffic duty. And the Swiss, Tidd, they're all criminals with num-bered bank accounts. This French commissionaire sent me some papers that they'd found in Grue's hotel room. Gave the name of a Swiss bank. We enquired, of course, but they would tell us nothing. You can't trust a foreigner, Tidd.' The Chief Constable fixed his glare on the occupants of a nearby table, a man with a long red nose and a short-sighted woman who was directing a chocolate bun into her mouth with her little finger stretched out as a sort of rudder. 'I was born an Englishman, Tidd! I have lived an Englishman! I shall die an Englishman!'

'That's terrible!' whinged the woman.

'Has yon mon nae ambeetion?' muttered the man with the long red nose.

'I'll show you those papers, Tidd, when we get back to the station. I'd like to know what you make of them.'

'I've often wondered what became of Grue, sir.' Tidd sighed in satisfaction, chomping chocolate bun. 'Just clothes lying by a lake in Switzerland.'

'There can be no doubt about the gallant fellow's fate. The clothes of Potter, the arch-criminal, were found there too. It is certain that they plunged together to their doom, locked in mortal combat. There are fearful falls there, Tidd, you know.'

Dilsie was back at their table with the bill. She sneezed. Late nights in haystacks.

'Reichenbach! Yes, that's the name.' The Chief Constable counted out money and punctiliously exact.

Dilsie sneezed again and coughed. She gathered up the money, popped a pastille in her mouth. 'Fo' cough.'

'And a very good afternoon chew,' responded the Chief Constable.

'Come, Tidd, there is work to do.'

At the police station the Chief Constable found the file and brought out the papers that the commissionaire had sent. 'See what you make of this, Tidd. It baffles me.'

Tidd scanned the sheets. He held some up to the light. 'I

think I have a clue,' he said and read through the material more carefully.

Spanish Ambassador at Genoa to Their Majesties:

No Admiral Columbus known here. Try Geneva.

Constantly in financial difficulties, Columbus turned his hand to anything that would earn him an honest peseta.

Dear Mr Columbus,

Many thanks for sending us your story. Your imaginative account of what befell a young Englishwoman in Spain is impressive and we would certainly have considered publication were we not overstocked with similar material. Every ship that bears its cargo of frustrated Englishwomen in search of a Latin lover returns laden with MSS recounting their experiences.

We are shortly to release *Topless in Cadiz*, which we have favoured because the bed into which the authoress leaped on disembarking was that of the *head* waiter. Whilst Spain may justly expect every waiter to do his duty, England has certain standards too.

Could you write again, but from a waiter's point of view? You might discover a whole new world of experience. We shall be pleased to hear from you.

Ivor Glugg, POTT BOOKS

Reversed Sir,

Chris Columbus, an old fiend of yoors, has appled to be our Porter. Was Chris yoor filosofy teecher as what he claims? And did he play rugger for Florrens RC? From where I am sat Chris seems not quite out of the top draw. My colleeg in Lisbon, Trevor Wigan, says

Chris upset one of his lecherers there and spoiled his lunch, what was a Mr Toscanelli and comes from yoor town, Trev says. I am HM Culcheral Attishoo here and needa good strong man behind me.
I have a social position to keep up.

>Howard Bootle, Rectum,
>English Culcheral Centaur, Benidorm

Dear Mr Bottle,

Mr Savonarola no longer with us. Sent your letter to English clergyperson in Monte Carlo. Heard things about English schools. Write briefly. Hands blistered chopping wood. Drowning better. RCs don't play that game here. Just let me catch anyone in the social position!

>Toscanelli
>Grand Inquisitor and President of Florence FC

>*from the Embassy Church, Monte Carlo*

My dear Bootle,

Yours to the late Mr Savonarola: I do not know Mr Columbus. I have such a thick head. Last Saturday when I came home the drab had washed my room and the bedchamber was all wet, and I was forced to go to bed in my own defence, and no fire. I was sick on Sunday and now have a swinging cold. I detest washing of rooms. Can't they wash them in a morning, and make a fire, and leave open the windows? I slept not a wink last night for hawking and spitting, and now everyone has colds.

>L. Gaiters, Archdeacon.

from the Embassy Church, Monte Carlo

My dear Columbus,

Of course I remember you! And now you have written a book! I write plays myself. I wonder if you could interest your publisher? My latest one is set on a bullockless space-wagon travelling to the moon. I have reached the point where Captain Gaiters moves into superwhack. Enter drab with mop. Gaiters liquidises her with his heavy water pistol.

And you are going for a sail! I have it in mind to go to Capri myself. Maybe that nice Mr Toscanelli who wrote about you would join me. It would be an opportunity to discuss the validity of English orders. I believe him to be sympathetic to the Anglican position for he concluded his letter with the salutation 'Up yours'.

No, we do not at present need another curate. But our business is likely to expand if they ever set up an English embassy here.

L. Gaiters, Archdeacon

I might have expected such ingratitude, da Vinci. It was the same when I saved your studio from the floods. You went off in a panic to invent a submarine while I got it all mopped up, despite the interference of your drab. I hope you still carry half a dozen pencils sharpened at both ends and in the middle, as I told you to.

C. Columbus, Assistant Waiter,
Venta de Delicias.

Dear Mr Glugg,

Your tip that I try writing from a waiter's point of view is the best tip I have yet had. Pending completion of my new novel, *Tipless in Córdoba*, I send my play, *Pig-power to Pluto*. I have experimented with methane gas and it works.

> Christopher Columbus, Head Waiter,
> Venta de Delicias.

(It is clear that the unknown compiler of the documents has been assiduous in bribery of drabs and varlets. But now the pace thickens. As rumour spread, lights burned late in the Chancelleries of the Powers and their agents coursed toward Córdoba.)

Secret to His Excellency.

Obedient to your Excellency's commands, I have proceeded with all haste and now less than six weeks after leaving Paris I am on the frontier of Spain. Always the élan! But triumphalmentally I report my discoveries. It is by pigeon post that the savage Sots in Edinburgh communicate with their agent in Córdoba. And, Excellency, I know who is the master spy of the perfidious English!

From a pigeon pie in Poitiers I withdrew a piece of paper which carried this message: 'Postage Doo. Yon mon Columbus has his boaties and deil a ane is Clyde-built. Is that no terrible! And so is Spanish whusky, nae better nor Scottish wine. Ah'll be glad tae be back in Edinburry. Tam Poco, the Doocote, Córdoba.'

In the country of the Dordogne, where English robbers live in gloomy splendour, I heard them speak of Oasanound. This says Oasanound and that says Oasanound and what says Oasanound about the other? This Oasanound commands even the most arrogant English, his name spoken in the hushed shouts of English awe, a person of the most complete authority amongst them, yet unknown to us. Their master spy, Excellency!

(unsigned)

Frae Ma Muckleness in Edinburgh tae Tam Poco

Your bonny doo got ate in Poitiers. Dinna use doos nor naething edible across France.

Wha pee.

(Editor's note: this is Scottish for 'what a pity'.)

You'll get no testimonial from me, Columbus. You were the most inaccurate operator of a mechanical writing machine in Milan. Only an econonic miracle got my bullockless-wagon factory in operation after your assistance. I hope you do the same thing for that fellow D. Troit.

Leonardo da Vinci.

Principal Eunuch to Deputy Assistant Eunuch:

Throw all these Fatimas in the Bosphorus. We don't know which has been offering my job to a Wop called Columbus.

Secret Jones to Less Important Jones:

Smokeless fuel unfair to working man. Sell all you can and join protest delegation of miners at Hilton Hotel, Marbella.

Secret Jones to Top Secret Jones:

Miners now all employed as waiters. Send bibles and harpstrings. Tell wife sell goats. Don't send wife.

Secret to His Lordship:

The Admiral has sailed, everyone shouting with excitement, each ship on its own course with frequent changes of direction but without signal of intention. Just as the Spanish do when walking in the streets. There were cries of 'Why don't you look where you are going, *puerco*!'

'Luff, Bosun, Luff!'

'Yare, O'Hooligan, Yare!'

''Tis 1492, sor!'

'Baffling, eh, Tidd?'

'Yes sir, and yet . . .' Tidd selected a sheet and folded it, following certain former folds. He held it up. 'A paper dart, sir!'

'By Jove!' The Chief Constable took it and made trial motions, then launched it into flight. It circled the room once, then flew through the open window. They leaned out to watch it. It floated gracefully toward the canal, then stopped abruptly in mid-flight and dropped to earth. Tidd made another. 'They've all been paper darts, sir!' Tidd launched it and it followed the same course. They folded in a frenzy and launched till all were gone. Below the window the side of the canal was littered with paper darts.

Tidd crossed his legs. Uneasily he looked round for a calendar.

'What day is it, sir? What's the date?'

'The third of August. Why, that's the day Columbus sailed!'

'We shouldn't have had that second pot of tea, sir. The third of August is also Ethelralda's Eve!'

No more will be told of Grue and Potter. The lives of the rich are never interesting.